Lyons took out his Atchisson. The young soldier gasped.

"What is that rifle?" the soldier asked.

Lyons described his crowd-killing device. "This is an Atchisson selective-fire assault shotgun. Loaded with a mix of steel shot, I can put out over four hundred projectiles in less than a second and a half. By changing mags, I can put out one thousand slugs in less than seven seconds."

The soldier's eyes bugged.

"Want one?" Lyons smiled.

The soldier nodded.

"Not yet," Lyons said. "Right now, this is my gun and my war. Nazis, Commies, pirates—*I pull the trigger on them all!*"

"Goes beyond law to true justice.
First in sales and popularity!"
—*West Coast Review of Books*

Mack Bolan's
ABLE TEAM

Mack Bolan's
PHOENIX FORCE

MACK BOLAN
The Executioner

ABLE TEAM
AN EXECUTIONER SERIES

Kill School

Dick Stivers

A GOLD EAGLE BOOK FROM

WORLDWIDE

TORONTO • NEW YORK • LONDON • PARIS
AMSTERDAM • STOCKHOLM • HAMBURG
ATHENS • MILAN • TOKYO • SYDNEY

First edition December 1983

ISBN 0-373-61209-5

Special thanks and acknowledgment to
G.H. Frost for his contributions to this work.

Printed in Canada

1

"A gang of assassins from the Popular Liberation Forces will attack Roberto Quesada tomorrow."

As a radio blared out staccato messages between the army posts guarding Highway 7 from San Miguel to the southeast border of El Salvador with Honduras, Lieutenant Guillermo Lizco of Las Boinas Negras stood at attention while he waited for his commander to respond to his statement. An elite unit of American-trained commandos, Las Boinas Negras, Black Berets, served in Morazan province; specializing in long-range reconnaissance and patrol, the unit often intercepted guerrilla kill teams terrorizing the community leaders and civic employees of remote mountain villages.

The guerrillas feared the lieutenant's unit. If guerrillas entered one of his ambushes, they died or became prisoners. But only those with weapons. Sometimes the guerrillas forced the local campesinos to carry their supplies. On more than one occasion, Lieutenant Lizco and his soldiers had only fired one shot each from their rifles. All the armed guerrillas in a group dropped, dead or seriously wounded, leaving the campesinos and the unarmed guerrilla sympathizers standing among bodies. Though the sympathizers disappeared into the torture chambers and mass graves of San Salvador, the Black Berets returned the campesinos to their villages. This gained the respect of the local people, who were accustomed to indiscriminate firefights and death-squad assassinations, and earned their support. Increasingly, campesinos and landowners and embittered leftists brought Lieutenant Lizco information on guerrilla operations.

As if he had not heard the lieutenant, the commander swirled coffee in a cup while he studied a relief map of the province. The contour lines infolded and twisted into an abstract design of near-infinite complexity to suggest the thousands of mountain ridges and valleys and rivers of Morazan.

"I received the information from a hotel clerk who overheard," Lieutenant Lizco added. "He knows they are PLF."

Lieutenant Lizco referred to the Popular Liberation Forces, a Stalinist group that admitted links with Cuba and the Soviet Union. Unlike the rebel forces who hoped for eventual reconciliation of the nation after victory, the Popular Liberation Forces fought a war of annihilation. They took no prisoners in their assaults on isolated army positions, putting bullets through the heads of captured soldiers or hacking fifteen-year-old draftees to death with machetes. They dispatched assassins to silence Salvadorans—conservatives, liberals, union leaders, socialists, Marxist utopians—who spoke of peaceful reform or a revolution ending without the creation of a "People's Soviet State." And they preached the doctrine of revenge: all Salvadorans who failed to join the People's Army faced execution after the Triumph.

Outside the mud-walled, bullet-pocked farmhouse where the Black Berets made their barracks and offices, the diesel generator sputtered and stopped. Both soldiers reflexively looked out the sandbagged window to the scorched cornfields. A midday attack? Guerrillas always sabotaged generators first, to cut off the lights and radios. But the officers saw no guerrillas advancing across the fields. No autofire cracked the quiet of the overcast afternoon. As their eyes searched the perimeter, the generator resumed its monotonous drone.

Finally turning to Lieutenant Lizco, the commander's exhausted, expressionless eyes examined the twenty-two-year-old junior officer. The commander glanced to the doorway to the other room. The lieutenant stepped to the door and looked out. The clerk had left the room that served as a unit office. Only then did the commander ask, "Quesada is a friend of yours?"

"No!" Lieutenant Lizco sneered.

"Perhaps his guards will protect him," the commander suggested. He turned away. Adding another cube of sugar to his coffee, he stared out at the black clouds bringing an early end to the afternoon. Lizco did not allow the silence to deny his point.

"It is an opportunity to stop a gang of assassins," he said.

The commander turned to him again. "Quesada is one of the fourteen. We cannot touch him."

For a moment the lieutenant did not comprehend his commander's words. Then he blurted, "No. I mean... I mean the Communists—"

"Oh, of course. The *Communist* terrorists." The commander nodded. "I was confused. I am confused. Perhaps I misunderstand you. You will risk your life, the lives of your men to protect that... butcher?"

"No. I will kill the assassins. This time they attack Quesada, but the next time...a teacher, a mayor, a soldier, perhaps farmers who want to vote. But it is convenient that they attack Quesada, for if I am too late to save him, I will not cry."

With a quick laugh, his commander granted the request. "Go. Assemble your squad. God grant you luck. But do not hurry, understand me?"

Laughing also, the lieutenant snapped a salute and left the offices. In the farmyard, Lieutenant Lizco looked up at the black sky. The overcast blocked the tropical sun. From the west, a wall of black churning clouds swept in from the Pacific.

The approaching storm confirmed the reports from the American weather satellites. Tonight would be another night of high winds and torrential rains.

No light planes, no helicopters would fly tonight.

WIND-DRIVEN RAIN BEAT the branches and fronds above Lieutenant Lizco and his men. All through the night, the winds of the violent storm had torn branches from the trees. Flowing rainwater became flowing mud as the steep hillside eroded. Silt covered their boots and camouflage fatigues. When their shallow fighting holes filled with black water that stank of rotting forest debris, the lieutenant and his squad put their weapons and ammunition on the rocks and branches around them. But they held their positions on the hillside. Only the lieutenant moved, leaving the shallow ditch he had gouged in the rocky soil to crawl from man to man, checking the seven men in his ambush squad.

Lieutenant Lizco peered across the valley to the lights of the Quesada plantation. One of the largest coffee *fincas* in El Salvador and the largest and most profitable in the province of Morazan, the plantation spread across the hillsides and fields of a valley in the foothills of the Cordillera Cacaguatique Coroban. With the heat of the tropical sun tempered by the altitude, the hills' fertile soil and year-round streams created a perfect location for the production of high-quality coffee.

Yet the valley had not been developed until twenty years before, when the Salvadoran government received a low-interest loan from the United States Agency for

International Development. With American money, road crews improved the road to San Francisco Gotera to make it a highway capable of carrying diesel semi-trucks loaded with tons of coffee. The remote valley suddenly had value. The Quesadas, one of the Fourteen Families who had controlled El Salvador throughout the three centuries following the Spanish Conquest, took title to the land. They paid a national-guard commander to massacre the campesino communities farming the valley, then the family developed the land for the production of coffee—clearing the fertile valley, building roads, laying out irrigation systems. After the coffee plants matured, the Quesadas exported millions of dollars worth of coffee each year to wholesalers in Europe and North America.

The *finca* had a grid of roads interconnecting the fields and warehouses. Elegant gardens lush with flowers and tropical fruit surrounded the sprawling complex of homes and apartments housing the individual families of the extended Quesada family. A reservoir and hydroelectric generator provided power for the streetlights and homes and equipment and concentric circles of electric fences that protected the family. A strip of open ground along a stream provided space for seasonal laborers to make shacks for their families during the harvest. An outer perimeter of barbed-wire fences and watchtowers, patrolled by the Quesada militia, protected the family and their vast *finca* from the guerrillas operating in the mountains of Morazan.

The barbed wire also imprisoned the migrant workers. Once inside the gates of the plantation, the campesinos left the twentieth century behind. The Quesadas ruled their *finca* as a feudal state. For three dollars a day, the campesinos began picking coffee before light and continued until dark, the militia enforcing the quick pace of the work with fists and kicks and sticks. The workers slept in cardboard shacks, and tents made of plastic scraps. Injuries went untreated. Children splashed in the muddy stream and died of pesticide poisoning. A Quesada store sold beans and canned food to the workers at prices calculated to take back the few dollars the Quesadas paid in wages. If workers complained of the abuse or the deaths of their children or the low wages and expensive food, their corpses joined the bones of Indians and mestizos who had first farmed the valley.

In case of a revolt of the campesinos or an assault by insurgents, a private airfield ensured the immediate arrival of troops. And the prefab hangars housed several private planes. The Quesada militia had mounted machine guns and bomb-release mechanisms on two of the planes. They regularly dropped twenty-gallon cans of gasoline mixed with concentrated insecticide on bands of suspected guerrillas. Ignitors sparked an explosion of flame and choking, sooty smoke that caused convulsions and lung hemorrhages.

But primarily, the airfield and private planes provided safe transportation for the family's most important members—such as the colonel. In good weather, family aircraft shuttled between the plantation and their mansions in San Salvador, avoiding any chance of skirmishes or assassination along the highways linking the *finca* to the capital. The light planes also carried vital supplies—weapons, ammunition, French whores, liquor, cocaine and videocassettes of North American television.

This morning, the storm and unnaturally violent winds had grounded all planes and helicopters.

Lieutenant Lizco looked down at the landscape graying with the first light of day. El Niño, he thought.

The shift in a sea current somewhere in the Pacific Ocean had caused climatic changes throughout the Americas. California enjoyed a mild winter and a long, cool spring. Mexico suffered drought. Guatemala experienced strange incidents of two-hundred-kilometer-per-hour jet streams descending from the stratosphere to rip through the countryside and cities. Hundreds died in Peru and Ecuador when torrential rains washed away *pueblos*, and avalanches of mud buried entire highways.

It is a warning from God, the lieutenant thought. *He can change the currents of the ocean, deny the life-giving rains, or send floods down on our countries. If we do not stop the atrocities and massacres, if we do not stop the injustice and hypocrisy, He will end this world and begin again.*

And the trial and punishment of Colonel Roberto Quesada would remove one offense to God from His earth.

Now, after twelve hours of waiting, the lieutenant watched the road for Colonel Quesada. He glanced at the road snaking through the foothills and forested valleys, but he did not take his binoculars from their case. The headlights of the trucks would announce Quesada.

As the day came, the shadowy forms of the mountains became landscapes of undulating green. Black storm clouds obscured the mountain peaks and swirled through gorges. Gusts of wind whipped the trees of the forest from side to side. The swaying branches created a pointillistic panorama of seething fertility and life.

The lieutenant stared at the beauty of El Salvador. At moments such as this, after nights without sleep, his fatigue and fear and adrenaline heightening his emotions, he loved his El Salvador with an intensity beyond simple military esprit or mere patriotism. For a mo-

ment, he surrendered his identity to the embrace of the
earth of El Salvador, the warm rain drumming on his
back becoming the blood drumming in his ears, his flesh
merging with the warm mud, his eyes and what his eyes
saw becoming inseparable. All became one: his dark
skin, his Olmec-Nahua-Spanish face, his European
name, his Indian heritage and his twentieth-century
hopes—the earth of Cuscutlan-El Salvador received him
as the faithful son it had created, Indian and Spanish,
sometime poet and dreamer and full-time commando....

A hiss from his nearest soldier startled him. Lieutenant Lizco realized he must have slept with his eyes open.
Now the storm clouds glowed silver with the sun. He
looked down to the road.

Trucks approached.

What the lieutenant saw confirmed the information
he had gathered in the preceding months.

The first truck was a four-wheel-drive Toyota Land
Cruiser with a whip antenna. It served as the point
vehicle. The militiamen inside watched for guerrilla
roadblocks and ambushes, the radio always on, the
microphone at hand to instantly transmit warning to the
other trucks following a kilometer behind. They also
had the duty of finding any land mines placed by guerrillas in the road. The second and third trucks, both armored Silverados, identical in year and color and trim,
stayed in the tracks of the Toyota's oversized tires. Colonel Quesada rode in the second or third truck, unseen
behind the gray-tinted windows. No guerrilla could aim
an antitank rocket at one of the Silverados with confidence of hitting the fascist colonel.

The trucks moved as fast as the mud-slick asphalt of
the road permitted.

To his sides, despite the drumming of the rain and

wind-lashing branches, the lieutenant heard the faint clicks of weapons going off safety as his men prepared to counterstrike the Communist assassins.

The soldiers watched the roadside for the Communists. This section of road, so close to the gates of the *finca*, offered the ideal opportunity for an ambush with rocket-propelled grenades. Following the folds of the mountains until the hillsides sloped into the valley, the road ran straight for the last few hundred meters to the gate. Flat expanses of truck-rutted mud created a trap. If the convoy swerved from the road, the mud would stop the trucks. If Quesada and his bodyguards stayed on the road and returned fire while they waited for rescue by the *finca* militia, the mud flats would become a kill zone. Only a hundred meters away, the forested hillsides could hide machine guns and rocket teams and snipers.

Finally taking his binoculars from the case, Lieutenant Lizco focused on the last Silverado, hoping to see through the windshield. Did Quesada ride inside? The high-powered optics revealed only silhouettes. Then the lieutenant watched the gate. A militiaman, rifle slung over his shoulder and walkie-talkie clipped to his belt, pushed open the steel-and-barbed-wire gates. In the watchtower, another militiaman casually held an M-16 as he watched the approaching convoy.

The point truck left the winding curves. The lieutenant looked to his soldiers. They shouldered their rifles and grenade launchers. The unit's sniper put his eye to the scope on his match-grade G-3 rifle while the spotter swept the scene with binoculars.

In the quiet of the rainswept morning, they heard the Silverados shift into high gear and accelerate into the straightaway. The lieutenant refocused his binoculars on the gate. He hoped to see one of the guards salute.

Perhaps Quesada would wave to his militiamen. Perhaps, once inside the *finca*, the lead truck and the Silverado carrying only the bodyguards would take a different road while Quesada sped in his Silverado to his luxurious home in the center of the valley.

No rocketflashes came from the mountains. No machine guns fired on the convoy. The lieutenant watched as the trucks roared across the last straightaway. The drivers screeched the trucks' brakes to slow for the series of speed bumps. Once they passed through the gate, they accelerated to a hundred kilometers per hour.

As his men muttered curses and gathered their equipment, the lieutenant kept his binoculars on the trucks inside the plantation. The lead truck—the Toyota Land Cruiser—turned onto a side road. But both Silverados continued directly to the gardens and homes of the Quesada family.

Lieutenant Lizco returned his binoculars to its case. He had not determined which truck carried Colonel Quesada, but he had confirmed several other important details. Though his soldiers cursed the informant who had misled them and condemned them to an all-night wait in the storm for nothing, Lieutenant Lizco considered his unit's operation a success.

No Communist assassins had waited for the fascist convoy, contrary to what the lieutenant had told his commander. Lieutenant Lizco had lied. True, an informant did tell the lieutenant of the colonel's rare overland commute to the *finca*. Only a few times in recent years had the weather forced the colonel or any of the other members of the family to risk the highways; now, in this year of strange weather when God sent violent storms to warn of His wrath, when weather denied the Quesadas their inviolate passage through the skies, the family would take the highways more often.

No Communist assassins lay in wait today. But soon the lieutenant himself hoped to ambush Quesada. He would not murder Quesada. He would kidnap him for the humiliation of public trial and judgment in the courts of the United States.

The lieutenant lay in the mud watching Colonel Quesada, the fascist murderer of Salvadorans and North Americans, race to the safety of his fortified estate.

That night, wearing the casual fashions of a Salvadoran playboy, with forged papers concealing his identity, Lieutenant Lizco carried his information far to the north, to San Francisco, California, to set in motion the relentless process of justice.

2

Electric fans created a wind of humid, polluted air through the improvised dojo. In sweaty T-shirts and homemade karate pants, two lines of ghetto boys—and one girl—practiced the rising-block defense against a punch to the face. A line stepped forward in attack, and a second line stepped back as the individuals defended themselves. Isador "The Izz" Goldman, a New York Police Department detective, went from child to child, correcting stances, watching moves, demonstrating correct techniques. He spoke English, Spanish and French to the class of North American and Jamaican blacks, Eastern European whites and Central Americans.

Rosario Blancanales and Carl Lyons served as demonstration subjects. In their sweat-yellowed *gis*, the two Stony soldiers waited as Izz Goldman called the students together and explained the next technique.

"Now defense becomes attack. Use the same upward blocking motion, but instead of deflecting the punch up and away, break the arm. Like this—"

Goldman motioned Lyons forward. Goldman had invited his buddy Rosario to the karate class and Rosario had brought this ex-cop with the impassive face and expressionless eyes. Making the ritual bow to his opponent, Goldman then waited as the blond man stepped forward in an exaggerated and slow punch.

Snapping his left forearm up, Goldman hit Lyons's

wrist hard with the bony edge of his forearm. The students asked to see the move again.

"Mr. Goldman. Do you hit only the wrist?"

"Is there a nerve there, Mr. Goldman?"

"If you hit it hard, will it really break?"

Repeating the same attack several times, Goldman struck the ex-LAPD officer's arm again and again. His eyes half-closed, expressionless, the blond man attacked on cue without flinching or holding back. Finally Goldman sent the students back to their practice. Lyons returned to tutoring a group of beginners.

Goldman went to his Puerto Rican friend, Rosario. "What's with lizard eyes? Doesn't your friend have any nerves?"

"What do you mean?"

"Like pain nerves. I must've hit him ten times in the same place and he doesn't even blink. Like looking a snake in the face."

"That's the way he is," Blancanales answered. He glanced over to Lyons. Lyons patiently demonstrated the technique of advancing in stance, knees flexed, feet sliding, eyes focused straight ahead. "That's the way he is now. Recently he lost a partner—more than a partner. He's still in mourning."

"Oh, yeah. Know about that. Tough. But that's the job."

"She was more than a partner. Looked like love and marriage. And then she was gone."

"Yeah, can imagine that."

"Not really," Blancanales corrected his New York buddy. "You don't know how broken up he is. You see, it was his fault—"

"What?"

"In a way. She was hurt and he tried to stop her from making the bust. Left her behind while we went to take the bad guys. She got pissed and did something wrong and went straight into it. If he hadn't gotten protective, she'd be alive.''

Across the converted basement, Lyons attempted to explain the principle of tension-nontension to a ten-year-old boy with the almond eyes and blue black hair of a Central American mestizo.

"All your strength must go outward...." Lyons exaggerated his front stance to emphasize his words. "But the strength cannot stop you from moving, and you must move with your legs strong. Then if your leg is kicked—as in an attack to your knee—nothing happens."

The boy tried to hold his leg muscles tense while he slid through steps. His rigid legs moved in awkward jerks. Lyons shook his head. "Relax. You can't move like that—"

"You say I should keep my legs strong. But if I keep them strong, I can't walk."

"Practice it every day. Your legs will be strong and your stance will be strong. Then you'll understand what I'm saying."

"Hey, social workers!"

Lyons looked up to see Gadgets Schwarz, the Able Team electronics specialist, standing on the steps. Tanned, wearing slacks and open-collared sport shirt, the ex-Green Beret looked like an off-season tourist.

"Got a man who wants to talk to you...." Gadgets motioned up the stairs behind him. "A man from Dee Cee."

Lyons answered with a nod. He turned to the mestizo boy. "Practice. In a year it will be easy."

"You will teach me? You come back for next class?"

Glancing to his waiting partners, Lyons shrugged. "Maybe."

The boy turned away, disappointed. Lyons crossed the varnished plywood of the basement dojo to the stairs.

"How's the Ironman?" Gadgets asked.

"Never better," he lied, his eyes hooded, revealing nothing of his grief.

"Ready to work?"

"Why not?"

"That's my man. Up there."

As they went up the stairs, Lyons looked back to see Izz Goldman dividing the students into advanced and beginner groups. Two advanced boys bowed, then sparred in awkward freestyle. The deep voice of Andrzej Konzaki turned Lyons's head.

"What you doing in this neighborhood, gringo?"

Lyons stepped up to the pavement. New Yorkers crowded the sidewalks. The unseasonably warm night throbbed with rhythm of Puerto Rican music blasting from a record store.

"I'm learning Spanish."

"Looks like you're training your own gang down there."

Blancanales answered the joke. "They're all honor students. *A*'s and *B*'s."

"And what do they get for it?" Lyons asked rhetorically. He sat on the concrete stoop of a tenement. In his white karate pants and clinging sweat-soaked shirt, with close-cut blond hair and golden tan, he stood out like neon against the old, soot-gray tenement. "I'll tell what they get, they get their heads kicked by the punks. So we're training them to... er, present a credible threat of counterforce. There it is. Why are you here?"

"Want to use your Spanish?"

"Where?"

"El Salvador."

Lyons and Blancanales exchanged glances. The Puerto Rican ex-Green Beret sat beside Lyons on the stoop and said, "Here's a quick Spanish lesson for you. The word for asshole in Spanish is *ano*. Like, *el ano del mundo*. Asshole of the world. It's spelled S-a-l-v-a-d-o-r."

"Quit the lip," Konzaki told Blancanales. "A straight answer."

Lyons shook his head. No.

"Hey, Ironman," Gadgets jived. "You dig it down south. Forests, mountains, papayas, tropical showers. Just like a vacation in Hawaii, except in Spanish."

"Just like a vacation in Dachau," Lyons answered. "Except in Spanish."

"Gentlemen," Konzaki pronounced, switching from his Marine voice to the voice of a capitol spokesman. "You are disparaging a democratically elected government attempting to reform a feudal nation while fighting a civil war."

"You believe that?" Lyons asked.

"No," Konzaki said, "but it sounds good."

"Then plug in your headphones when you talk that shit," Lyons countered bitterly. "I don't want to hear it."

"Then hear this, you limp-wristed bleeding-heart pinko liberal—" Konzaki swore.

"The Ironman? A pinko?" Gadgets asked incredulously.

"You want Quesada?" fumed Konzaki. "Remember Colonel Roberto Quesada, recently of Miami Beach, Florida? Wanted for the murder of David Holt and Alfred Lopez?"

"I remember the FBI went out with a warrant twenty-four hours after we gave them the information."

"Now we got information. Where he is. How he travels. Times, routes, security details."

Lyons looked to his partners. Blancanales nodded. Gadgets grinned.

"The Ironman's interested all of a sudden," Gadgets said.

"What's the op?" Lyons asked.

"There are federal and state warrants on him," Konzaki told them. "If Quesada were to return to the United States, he would be subject to the courts of the United States of America."

"And no questions asked about how he came back," Gadgets added.

"Who knows about the mission?" Lyons asked.

"No one knows but you three."

"Then where'd the information come from? A box of Cracker Jacks?"

"A Salvadoran national gathered the information," Konzaki replied. "He flew to San Francisco and offered it to a Señor Rivera. You know him. Señor Rivera called the Justice Department and said he had information on a fugitive. As soon as Rivera identified himself, the department forwarded his call to Brognola's office. Only the Salvadorans and Hal know what the information is. No one else."

"What about your friends in the Agency?" Lyons asked, his voice cold.

"I don't work there anymore, Mr. Lyons," Konzaki stated. "Why would you think that Stony Man shares sensitive information with questionable allies?"

"I got no objections to flying south for a look-see," Gadgets told his partners.

"Maybe Quesada comes back," Blancanales told Konzaki, "maybe not."

Finally Lyons nodded. "This is it—standard equipment, civilian clothes and ten thousand dollars in hundreds."

"Why so much money?" Konzaki asked. "You'll have a liaison man to provide what you need."

"Maybe we'll have to buy our way out," Lyons told him. "I don't speak Spanish, but everybody understands hundred-dollar bills."

"I'll have to call Stony Man to confirm the cash," Konzaki answered.

"Call, don't call. I don't care. No cash, no go." Lyons left his partners without another word. He went down the stairs to the basement.

"What's with him?" Konzaki asked the other two men of Able Team.

"Since Flor got wasted," Gadgets started to explain, "that man is cold. I mean, *cold.*"

Blancanales continued the explanation. "Since Flor got wasted by a gang of crew cuts in suits with Agency equipment in an Agency car who identified themselves as agents of the United States government—"

"Not same lovable guy anymore," Gadgets added, trying to joke. "Tends to be sort of suspicious."

No one laughed.

In the basement dojo, Lyons returned to training the beginners in the basics of karate. The group of advanced students sparred under Goldman's supervision.

Two of the older boys demonstrated excellent free-style technique, sparring with full-speed punches and kicks but maintaining a polite distance from each other's body. None of the kicks or punches actually struck flesh.

Throwing a flurry of punches, one of the boys drove his opponent back, then aimed a hard straight kick at his solar plexus to take the victory. But his opponent skipped back, making distance from the kick, and crashed backward into the beginners. Lyons saw one of the older boy's heels accidentally slam into the calf of a young boy. The young boy—the student Lyons had spoken to earlier—cried out in pain and fell clutching his leg. Lyons went to him instantly.

"Is he hurt?" Goldman asked.

Lyons pushed up the cloth of the boy's homemade *gi*. The boy cried out again when Lyons examined his calf.

"He'll have a bruise. Limp for a few days."

Goldman pushed the gathered students back to their places. The class resumed. Lyons took the boy aside and massaged the knot forming in the boy's calf muscle.

"Is it broken?" the boy asked.

"If it was broken, you couldn't even limp. What's your name?"

"Milton."

"After the English poet?"

"My father taught English. He said Milton was a great poet."

"I wondered why your English was so good. You're lucky your father can help you. You can make more money in the United States speaking English and Spanish."

"I won't live here when I am old. I go back to Salvador."

"Then when you go back, you'll make more money. Smart kids who can speak languages make money wherever they go."

"My father said there can be no understanding if we do not know the language of other people."

"He's right," Lyons agreed, conscious of his own ignorance.

Words came quickly from Milton. Though he had not cried with the pain of his injured leg, now his eyes filled with tears. "On Sundays, he took me where the tourists were. We talked with many people, so I could

speak English. Sometimes, I was a guide. I went everywhere with Americans. I took them to the ruins. Where
my people lived before the Spanish came.''

"Good way to make money. Is your leg hurting
more? What's wrong?''

"I don't want money. I don't want to speak English.
I want to be with my father, to fight with my father.
So don't talk about money, mister.''

"Your father's fighting in El Salvador?'' Lyons
asked quietly, trying to calm the crying ten-year-old.
"Where?''

"Chalatenango. Where our village was. Until the
soldiers and the bombers came and massacred our village.''

"What soldiers? The guerrillas?''

Milton looked at Lyons with disbelief. "We don't
have airplanes. Only the rich have bombers.''

"Your father's a guerrilla?''

"He fights the soldiers. When I go back, I fight,
too. I will kill all the soldiers.''

"Not all soldiers are the enemy. What if I was a soldier? What if he was a soldier?'' Lyons nodded toward
Blancanales.

"But you're helping us. In Salvador, the soldiers
would kill you for helping us.''

Lyons smiled. "I don't think so.''

"You are not Salvadoran. You know nothing.''

A whistle came from the stairs. Lyons saw Gadgets
give him a thumbs-up sign. Lyons helped Milton to his
feet. The boy wiped his tears away and started back to
the beginners' group.

"Hey, Milton,'' Lyons called. "Quit for the
night.''

"No. I must learn fast. Then I go back. Until we kill
them all, the soldiers, the rich, the Spanish, we will

fight. They are all the enemy. If you were Salvadoran, you would know.''

Lyons gave the young boy a salute. ''Thanks for the advice.'' Then the North American ex-cop followed his partners into the New York City night.

3

"You're setting up this colonel to be kidnapped by foreigners," Lyons said to Lieutenant Lizco. "Why? You're both officers in the same army, fighting for the same country."

After leaving New York City on an Air Force jet, Able Team had stopped first in Washington, D.C., for equipment and cash from Stony Man. They continued to San Francisco to pick up Lieutenant Lizco. After refueling the jet, they flew south for El Salvador. Now the lieutenant briefed them—in the efficient and impersonal manner of a professional soldier—on the details of Colonel Quesada's security.

"Why?" The lieutenant considered the question.

Konzaki, the fourth North American at the jet's conference table, answered first. "Call it international cooperation. Quesada ordered the murders of United States citizens. And the lieutenant has the courage to bring that bastard to justice."

But Lyons's eyes never left the lieutenant. Without acknowledging Konzaki's answer, the ex-LAPD detective watched the Salvadoran. Gadgets picked up one of the aerial photos supplied by Stony Man and studied the concentric rings of security around the gardens and homes of the Quesada family. Blancanales glanced at his watch.

"ETA, four hours," Blancanales reminded his partners. "We should finish the briefing before we discuss the motivation of—"

"What do you know of my country?" the lieutenant asked Lyons.

"I know nothing," Lyons answered, remembering what the ten-year-old son of a guerrilla had told him in the New York City basement. Lyons waited for the lieutenant to continue.

The young soldier smiled. "A North American who admits his ignorance. Good. I will educate you very quickly.

"One. There is not one war in my country. There are many. The government against the guerrillas. The guerrillas against the people. The Communist guerrillas against the other guerrillas. The army against the politicians. The old generals of the army against the young officers and the progressive politicians. The young officers and progressives against the fascists in the government. The fascists and the Fourteen Families and the old generals against everyone who is not one of them.

"Two. I fight for the revolution. Not the revolution of Marx or Cuba or Russia or the United States—the revolution of October 1979, when the young officers of the army decided to take the future of Salvador away from the families and the generals. My brother and my father joined the revolution and fought for land reform and justice and opportunity for our people. My brother fought the Communists who wanted no reforms. My father fought the fascists who wanted no reforms. My father and brother died. Now I fight the enemies of the revolution, the Communists and the fascists who have stopped the reforms.

"Three. The animal Quesada is not a soldier. He bought his commission. He never served Salvador. Only the families. He never carried a rifle. He never fought as a soldier, man to man with the enemy. He sends out death squads to torture and murder Salvadorans who only want to live as men and women in a modern country instead of as slaves to the families. His squads killed my father and my aunt and my cousins. Perhaps one of his assassins killed my brother, I don't know. When North Americans interfered—the reporter and the lawyer—he killed them, too.

"Four. Quesada is not Salvadoran. He has estates in Miami and Spain. He invests his money in Europe. Salvador is where he grows coffee. He cares nothing for Salvador or the people.

"He is my enemy. He is more than an enemy. He and his family and the other families led Salvador into this chaos and slaughter. A campesino becomes a guerrilla after he sees his village massacred. A politician goes and fights in the mountains after the death squads take his children. But they are Salvadorans and after the war, when there is justice, they will help rebuild Salvador. But the families? They have run away to Spain where they live in villas and talk about the good days, before the Communists came from Cuba."

"That sounds great," Lyons commented. "So why don't you pull the trigger on him?"

Lieutenant Lizco shook his head. "Then he would be only another rich man murdered by the Communists. Your president would call him a martyr for democracy. But if he is tried in the United States, with all the cameras of the world on him, he will be shown as the fascist that he is. The Quesadas and all the other families will be exposed. The people of your country and the world will learn the truth about the war in my country and why we fight. That is why I want your help. Do you understand me?"

"The politics don't count," Gadgets said, looking up from the aerial photos. "We'll just snatch that Nazi punk and drag him back. Give him a starring role on the six-o'clock news."

Blancanales spoke carefully. "The politics of your country cannot be our concern. It would be wrong for me to even comment on what you have told me. However, I can say that we are fortunate to find someone who'll help us bring a murderer to justice."

"Justice and shame," Lieutenant Lizco corrected. "I could have killed him many times. But death is too quick for him. Trial in the United States is what must be done."

Konzaki cut off the unnecessary talk. "Please continue with your briefing, Lieutenant."

"Yes, yes.... As you can see—" the lieutenant pointed to a twenty-by-thirty-inch aerial photo of the Quesada plantation in Morazan province "—infiltration of the *finca* is not possible. First there is the perimeter with the towers and dogs and infrared scopes. Then the militia that patrols the *finca*. Then the second perimeter that guards the residences of the Quesada families—electric fences, with modern alarm systems. I succeeded in befriending a militiaman. He bragged to me of killing some guerrillas who came in with only knives and pistols. He said the detector system caught them—"

"What kind of detectors?" Blancanales asked.

Gadgets answered. "Could be magnetic. The steel of the pistols and knives, or even their ammunition or belt buckles, would've done them. But then again, the sensors could be audio, seismic, or photoelectric. Maybe even radar. If those Nazis are millionaires, they can afford whatever they want."

"True," the lieutenant said, nodding. "For that reason, I do not suggest an infiltration. Both the *finca* and the residence in the capital have too many guards, too many electronic devices. What I suggest is an ambush—"

"But you said he zips back and forth by plane," Gadgets interrupted.

"Yes. Except when the weather forces him to take the highway. Have you read of the strange weather? Usually the rains come gently. Every day, a little rain, then the sun comes. But this year, many storms. So when he can he flies, but often now he must take the highway. He travels in a group of three trucks. A truck in the lead, then two kilometers back, two trucks. If guerrillas attack the first truck, or if it hits a mine, the other ones escape."

"Why don't the locals hit this rich man?" Gadgets asked. "They see him cruising around in his convoy of battlewagons, they've got to know he's someone important."

"That is the risk of the highways," the lieutenant said. "But it is not uncommon to see two or three trucks together. People who must go to the villages travel in pickups like those. When the guerrillas strike, they risk counterattack by the army. Why should the guerrillas attack only a plantation manager or government clerk when they can attack a convoy of troops or gasoline or coffee trucks?"

"What do you think, Ironman?" Gadgets asked Lyons.

"Makes sense. So how long do we wait for a storm?"

"Only a few days. Look." The lieutenant pulled a satellite photo from under all the other photos and maps. The Comsat computer-enhanced photo showed the swirls of storms off the shores of Central America. "Soon, perhaps the day after tomorrow, another storm comes. If Quesada travels, he travels by road."

"And if he doesn't?" Lyons asked.

"We wait." The lieutenant pointed to the satellite photo. "There are many storms coming. Perhaps we wait a day, perhaps a week. I have waited many months to avenge my father. You can wait a week."

Gadgets nodded. "Got my vote. Pol, you willing to kill a few days?"

"We'll need standby transportation for the prisoner," Blancanales said, and looked at Konzaki.

"He's on his way to Honduras now," Konzaki said, referring to the Stony Man ace pilot, Jack Grimaldi. "You get Quesada to an airstrip and he's on his way back."

Blancanales nodded. "I'll go."

They looked to Lyons. His eyes expressionless, showing nothing, Lyons glanced at his partners. "Why not? Almost there already."

Gadgets laughed. "What enthusiasm! Not exactly gung ho on this one, are you?"

"You know what happened last time." Lyons looked out the port to the clouds and green lands of Central America below the jet. "We broke Quesada's gang. We got his address and passed the information to the Feds. And the Feds waited a day and a night before getting a warrant. You don't have to be Sherlock Holmes to figure what goes. That Nazi has friends we know nothing about and couldn't touch if we did. Chances are, we'll deliver him to the Justice Department and he'll be on the next flight back to El Salvador. 'So sorry, he escaped.'"

Lyons turned to his partners. "But we'll get him. We'll do our job. We will do whatever is necessary."

4

As the Air Force jet descended through clouds, Able Team looked out the ports to the vast flashing mirror of the Lago de Ilopango. Around the lake—actually the flooded crater of an ancient volcano—green fields checkerboarded the lush countryside. The clouds cast patches of darkness on the flatland fields. Brilliant sunlight on forests created scenes of luminescent green. To the southeast, the cones of volcanoes extended to the horizon.

"Wow," Gadgets gasped. "Amazing! What a postcard that would make."

Lieutenant Lizco laughed. "This is the first time you see my country? It is very beautiful. But when you learn the history, the five thousand years of cities and empires and peoples, then you will be very, very amazed."

Lining up on a runway, the jet dropped into a landing approach. The North Americans and the Salvadoran army officer took their seats and buckled their safety belts.

Despite the clouds of the approaching storm, the pilot glided down to a flawless landing. The jet taxied past the brilliant white and glass of the terminal to the white hangars at the far end of the airfield.

Everywhere on the blacktop, jetliners and private jets loaded and offloaded passengers and luggage. Gadgets pointed to the modern terminal.

"Things don't look very desperate. Could've bought a million rifles for the price of that place."

"Japanese money," Lieutenant Lizco told him. "General Romero wanted many tourists to come to our country. He built roads and hotels and the airport. But the people got nothing. And the war came down from the mountains. Now, I think only journalists use the airport. And they do not come to photograph beauty."

"No tourists?" Gadgets asked. "Look at all those tourists back there."

"They are Salvadorans. Returning from Miami and Los Angeles and New York."

Lyons watched a group of teenagers in designer jeans and silk shirts board a Lear jet. "Look at the kid in the tight pants. Doesn't your country have a draft or selective service?"

The lieutenant laughed cynically. "You expect the rich to fight for the privileges the rich enjoy? That is the duty of the poor. As it is in your country, yes?"

"No," Gadgets answered. "In Nam, I had a captain whose family was rich. Had gear from Abercrombie and Fitch in Manhattan. Shared his Chivas Regal with me. He was one brave dude. Lost a leg and eye trying to drag in a wounded grunt."

The Salvadoran apologized. "I am sorry. I should not assume your country is like mine."

"Then again," Gadgets added, "when the Army drafted all the poor kids and started calling in the rich kids, that's when the antiwar movement started. I saw thousands of rich kids on TV marching with NVA flags and posters of Uncle Ho-Ho, proclaiming the People's Republic of Yale."

"Do you know," the lieutenant mused, "that in my country's war, many of the Communist leaders are the sons and daughters of the rich. That is very strange, yes? A class contradiction, as the Marxists say."

The jet turned. Slowing, it eased into the shadowy interior of a hangar. A lurch signaled their arrival as the pilot hit the brakes for the last time. The lieutenant went to the cabin door.

"No more talk of politics," he announced. "I must arrange for our transportation to Morazan. It will take only a few minutes. Then we go."

A ramp clanked against the fuselage, and the door swung open. The lieutenant stepped out. Lyons leaned to Konzaki.

"While we put together our gear," he said, "go delay our friend. I want the Pol to be with him when he makes his calls."

"He's legit, Carl," Konzaki replied. "We checked him out. Excellent record at Fort Benning. We checked him all the way back to his high-school friends."

"You know who he's talking to? Did you check them? Did you check the telephone lines? Did you check—"

"All right, Carl, all right. I'm on my way." Konzaki gripped his aluminum canes and left as quickly as his plastic legs allowed. They heard him call out, "Lieutenant! One moment!"

Lyons leaned to Gadgets. "Got a minimike and a DF? I want that Lizco wired."

Gadgets faked a shocked expression. "But he's our friend! How could you suggest such a thing?"

"Because I don't trust—"

"Anybody," Gadgets finished the statement. He grinned as he took a hand-radio from the inside pocket of his sports coat. "Think I do?"

With a flick of a switch, the voices of Konzaki and Lieutenant Lizco came from the radio. "How exactly will you travel? Should the men change into casual clothes? Or should they wear coats and ties. I'm thinking about checkpoints. Perhaps they should wear their suits to impress the authorities."

Lyons laughed. "Okay. This is what we're going to do. The Wizard has him wired. We're going to listen to what he does and what he says."

LEAVING THE NORTH AMERICAN EX-MARINE, Lieutenant Lizco jogged from the hangar. Outside, he started to the far end of the airfield, where private planes clustered around other hangars and mechanical shops. He saw a gasoline tanker bumping along a service road. Sprinting a hundred meters, the lieutenant leaped onto the rear bumper and rode to the private planes.

In a row of charter aircraft, he saw the blue-and-white six-passenger Cessna his friend owned. Though Garcia, the owner-pilot, had been a trusted lifelong friend of his father's, the lieutenant had no intention of telling Garcia the identities of the three North American passengers he would carry this morning. As the truck slowed to a stop at a fuel pump, Lieutenant Lizco stepped off.

He jogged through the parked Pipers and Cessnas and Beechcrafts. The middle-aged, pot bellied Garcia stood at his plane supervising the work of a mechanic. Lieutenant Lizco stopped short. He picked up a bit of asphalt from the blacktop and flicked it.

Garcia turned. He recognized the young man. The lieutenant motioned to the rows of planes. Garcia nodded. As the Salvadoran army officer wove through the parked planes, Garcia spoke with the mechanic for a moment before leaving him. He started toward the hangars, then doubled back. He glanced around the airfield before joining the lieutenant in the shadow of a Beechcraft's wing.

"The journalists are here, Guillermo?" Garcia asked.

The lieutenant nodded. "Is there a problem with the plane?"

"Routine work. When do we go?"

"When will the plane be ready?"

"A few minutes. How do we do this?"

"They cannot be seen. If possible, I would not involve you. You risk your life and your family. But there is no other—"

"This is for your father? For Alicia? For Luis and Anna?" Garcia crossed himself as he spoke the names of the "disappeared." "What is the world without my friends? Without the children who laughed with my children? We must fight the assassins. If these journalists have the balls to expose Quesada and his gang, I would be a coward not to help them. It is an honor to take them to San Miguel. I am not afraid."

"Thank you. I will go make them ready. When your plane is finished, prepare to leave. I will bring them in a car."

He shook Garcia's hand and left. Watching the hangars and work sheds, the lieutenant dodged from plane to plane. No one saw him leave the pilot. At the end of the lines of parked aircraft, he cut across the blacktop to the access road. This time no trucks provided a ride.

Walking along the access road, he glanced at the hangars and trucks he passed. He could not allow anyone to observe him. A junior officer on leave had no reason to meet with North Americans. If a treasury agent or quardía officer or national-guard intelligence operative saw him with the North Americans and somehow identified him, he faced "disappearance": days of torture and mutilation in the basement of a police station, then the dumping of his faceless, sexless, anonymous corpse in a ditch or river, or on the desolate lava wasteland of El Playon.

To join the scattered bones of the thousands of unknown dead. . . . To join his father in the soil of a corrupt and ravaged country.

A light green Dodge sedan cruised slowly toward him. Rifle barrels extended from both rear-door windows. Keeping his hands in the open, the lieutenant continued his stride.

The Dodge slowed to a stop and waited. Mirrored sunglasses watched him, the faces of the four national-police officers impassive as stones. Inside the car, a police dispatcher's voice squawked in competition with the blaring voices and trumpets of a Mexican pop song. The lieutenant attempted to ignore the police.

"Halt."

Lieutenant Lizco waited as the doors flew open. The muzzle of a G-3 jammed into his ribs. He heard clicks as the policeman flicked the rifle's safety on and off. Behind him, another safety clicked off.

"Identification," a police sergeant demanded. He rested his right hand on his holstered .45 automatic and extended his left hand.

Opening his sports coat wide before he reached for his wallet, the lieutenant felt his hand shaking. Not with fear, but with rage.

How many guerrillas had these police created? How many young men and women despised their country and their government because of these...these.... The lieutenant did not want to use the word police. While he fought in Morazan, these middle-aged goons threatened and insulted and beat, sometimes raped or murdered the young people of the city.

"He is a lieutenant in the army," the fattest goon told the others. "Why are you here, soldier? The Communists are in the mountains."

"I need a plane to get back to my unit. If the Communists are in the mountains, why are you here?"

The fat sergeant laughed. "Subversives are everywhere. We search for them."

A policeman with a G-3 laughed. "Maybe we find a pretty one."

"Go, soldier."

Restraining himself from speaking again, the lieutenant walked away. His body tensed with the expectation of a bullet in his skull. He forced himself not to look back. When he heard the car doors slam, he allowed himself the luxury of anger, his rage becoming a long monologue of obscenities and curses. He glanced back to the Dodge as it continued to the hangars of the private planes.

"After the Communists, I fight you, pigs!"

MONITORING THE MINIMIKE, Blancanales translated the threat.

"Is he okay?" Gadgets laughed. He punched Lyons in the shoulder, his karate-hardened fist hitting a deltoid of iron. "I mean, is he okay? He's okay in *my book*."

Lyons's eyes narrowed to slits. "Disrespect for police officers indicates subversive tendencies...." Then the ex-LAPD detective laughed also. "All right, enter Lizco's name in *The Book of the Cool*."

Able Team had watched the young officer's encounter with the national police from a window in the aircraft hangar. The minimike had transmitted every word to Blancanales, who translated the words of the police, then the obscenities and threats of the lieutenant.

The lieutenant approached the hangar and the steel doors slid open. A North American technician, who Konzaki had told them had embassy security clearance, attached a truck's tow bar to the tail of the Air Force jet. Able Team turned their faces away as the technician pulled the jet from the cool darkness of the hangar.

"But," Lyons continued, "the minimike stays on him. How long is it good for, Wizard?"

"Indefinitely. I can switch it on and off to save the battery."

"Good. We'll go along with this kid. But all the identification we brought from Stony Man—the passports, the credit cards, the media identification—we can't use it."

"Carl, we need that identification to move through the country," Blancanales told his partner.

"That's why we've got the ten grand in cash. We'll buy forged ID. Chances are the Agency printed the identification for Stony Man. Which means every Nazi and death squad in the country has it. If we show it to a soldier or cop, they'll take us."

"The Central Intelligence Agency works for the United States," Blancanales countered. "Not the Salvadoran fascists."

"Oh, yeah? Who were those crew-cut types who killed—" Lyons's voice caught with an instant of grief "—who killed Flor?"

"Man, nobody knows about them," Gadgets broke in. "Just because they *look* Agency doesn't mean they *are* Agency. Could've been Russians, maybe Albanians. Could've been Martians for all we know."

"Quit the jive," Lyons told him. "I know."

Blancanales stopped their talk. "Here he comes."

The lieutenant stepped through the office door. He glanced to the truck towing the Air Force jet. When he saw no one observing him, he crossed to the North Americans.

"We go to Morazan. The plane waits."

The three Stony warriors took their heavy cases of weapons and gear.

IN THE TRUCK towing the Air Force jet, the blond, blue-eyed technician watched the three North Americans leave with the Salvadoran. He noted the obvious weight of the cases that the tall, hard-muscled men carried. Then the technician continued with his work. He towed the jet to the fuel station. While the Salvadoran workers refueled the plane, the tow-truck operator went to a telephone.

"This is Scott. They're here."

A Spanish-accented voice questioned him. "You are positive? Describe them."

"They match the photos. The Latin, the blond-haired Anglo, the dark-haired Anglo with the mustache. They arrived with the one without legs. In a jet. No company markings. A Salvo national took them away in a car."

"To where?"

"I don't know. They were very cautious, I couldn't overhear them. I attempted to plant a bug, but they never left their equipment for a second."

"What equipment?"

"Heavy, heavy suitcases. Oversized, long enough for rifles. I couldn't get any other information. They were all watching me."

A laugh came through the phone. "So now we will watch them."

5

Over the noise of the idling Cessna engine, they heard the small-arms fire. Gadgets went flat in the dust of the airfield. Lieutenant Lizco shouted to Garcia.

"Go! There is fighting!"

"But you? How will you escape?"

"It is already arranged! Go! Now!"

Garcia leaned across the seat and gave the lieutenant and the three "journalists" a salute. Then he jerked the cabin door closed. The engine roared. A sandstorm enveloped the four men as the Cessna pivoted. Bumping across the dirt airfield, the Cessna gained speed and lifted off.

The firing continued, somewhere to the north. Lyons took off his sunglasses and blew dust and grit off the lenses. He scanned the sunlit, forested mountains around them.

"No one's shooting at us," he commented as he stood up. He grabbed his equipment cases. "But things could change. Make distance."

The lieutenant grabbed one of the cases. He pointed to a hillside tangled with dense brush and second-growth pines. "There. I have a car hidden."

"Where are we?" Gadgets asked as they double-timed.

"North of Lolotiquillo."

"Great. Where's that?"

"North of San Francisco Gotera."

Gadgets laughed. "Oh, yeah? And where's that?"

The army officer did not stop to answer. Pushing through branches, he led them into the shadows of the hillside's trees. He set down the suitcase he carried. When the three North Americans joined him, he put out a hand for silence.

They waited, listening. Insects droned around them. In the distance, the rifle fire continued. The ripping noise of M-16s on full-auto answered the sharp booms of heavy-caliber battle rifles. The roar of an M-60 punctuated the firefight.

"M-60s and M-16s," Lyons guessed.

"Army?" Gadgets whispered.

The lieutenant nodded. "And guerrillas."

Other weapons roared in one disciplined explosion of autofire.

Blancanales glanced to his partners. "Those aren't M-60s. Cyclic rate's too fast."

"Sounds like a squad of G-3s to me," Lyons commented.

Gadgets flicked open the latch of his weapons case. "Don't sound like no brass-band reception. We're here. This is it."

They silently opened their cases. Stripping off their sports coats, Blancanales and Gadgets put on identical shoulder holsters. Both men carried silenced Beretta 93-Rs. The pistols represented the cutting edge of Beretta technology. A selective-fire sear mechanism triggered both single shots and 3-round bursts. An oversized trigger guard and a lever that folded down from under the barrel provided a secure two-hand grip. Slightly underpowered loads in their cartridges propelled steel-cored slugs at subsonic speeds for silent attacks.

From his case, Lyons took out his 4-inch-barreled

Colt Python. Undoing his belt, he put a holster at the small of his back.

Then he slipped into standard shoulder-holster rig for a nonstandard weapon: a Colt Government Model reengineered for silence. Redesigned and hand-machined by Andrzej Konzaki to incorporate the innovations of the Beretta autopistols, the interior mechanisms of the Colt no longer resembled what Browning had invented and patented. Like the Berettas, a fold-down lever and oversized trigger guard provided a positive two-hand grip. But it fired full-powered .45-caliber slugs, silent, in semiauto and three-shot burst modes. Lyons jammed in an extended ten-shot magazine, leaving the chamber empty. He checked the Allen screw securing the suppressor before holstering the weapon.

Able Team loaded their assault weapons. Gadgets snapped back the actuator of his CAR-15 to chamber a round. Blancanales loaded and locked his M-16/M-203 over-and-under hybrid assault rifle and grenade launcher. He slipped a 40mm high-explosive fragmentation grenade into the launcher. But he left the launcher tube uncocked. Lyons took out his Atchisson assault shotgun. The lieutenant tapped him on the shoulder.

"What is that rifle?" the Salvadoran asked.

Lyons gave a whispered description of the weapon. "Atchisson selective-fire assault shotgun. Twenty-inch rifled barrel. Slug sights with flip-up rear apertures for fifty and a hundred yards. Magazine holds seven rounds. Thumb fire-selector, safe, one-shot, three-shot, full-auto. And the shells—aluminum casings to eliminate the chance of a plastic shell melting in the chamber and fusing solid. Loaded with a mix of double-ought and number-two steel shot. I can put out over four hundred projectiles in less than a second and a half. Starting with a round in the chamber and changing mags, I can put out one thousand projectiles in less than seven seconds. One man fire-superiority, yes?''

Smiling, the lieutenant looked into the weapon cases. ''Do you have another?''

''Want one?''

Lieutenant Lizco nodded.

''Could be arranged. But not now.'' Lyons pulled back the Atchisson's actuator and slipped a round in the chamber. Then he jammed in a magazine. ''Where's that truck?''

''It is a car. Come. It is near.''

They eased through the brush with their heavy cases. In the distance, the autofire died away to occasional bursts and single shots. The shriek-roar and explosion of an RPG ended the firefight.

''That one's over,'' Gadgets told Blancanales. ''Sounds like the side with the ComBloc weapons won.''

''Not your war, Wizard. Nothing you can do.''

Lyons heard his partners. ''I'll do whatever I can,'' he said. ''Wherever I go, it's my war. Nazis, Commies, pirates—I pull the trigger on them all.''

''Tough talk, Ironman,'' Blancanales hissed. ''But you can't fight the world.''

''What have I been doing for the past few years?''

Gadgets laughed. ''That man talks the facts.''

''Here is the car.'' Lieutenant Lizco pointed to a tangle of brush.

They put down their cases and thrashed into the bushes. Living trees and brush had been cleverly bent and twisted to conceal the vehicle in living camouflage. As they pulled aside the branches, they saw camouflage sheeting.

The lieutenant slashed the sheeting with a pocket knife. They saw gleaming paint and a tinted window. Dragging the knife blade through the camou fabric, he cut the sheeting away from the front end of the luxury car.

"A Coupe de Ville?" Lyons asked, staring wide-eyed at the vehicle.

"I could not get a truck," the Salvadoran officer explained. "A rich politician would not risk the roads. It disappeared from the garage. . .and came here."

"We travel in style!" Gadgets jived.

Swinging open the door, the lieutenant tried the engine. It roared. He eased the Cadillac out of its camouflage. He flicked the electric lock switch. Able Team jerked open the doors and threw in their cases.

"Now where?" Lyons asked.

"South." The lieutenant guided the luxury car through the brush. He braked when he reached the airstrip. He took tape and a bundle of paper from the floor of the Cadillac. "Here. Tape these signs to the car. Hurry."

"Sure, sure." Lyons and Blancanales jumped out.

Opening the bundle, they found several bold lettered signs—red letters on the white paper—stating *Periodistas*.

"Newsmen," Blancanales translated.

Working fast, they taped the signs to the hood, the roof and the trunk. They jumped back inside.

"You think of everything," Lyons told the lieutenant.

"I have planned this for months."

Accelerating across the airstrip, Lieutenant Lizco fishtailed onto the gravel road. Ruts and bumps made the Cadillac rock like a boat. The Salvadoran drove from side to side on the road, avoiding muddy holes, sometimes steering up onto the bulldozed shoulder to avoid the worst ruts.

In the back seat, Gadgets explored the comforts enjoyed by the rich politician owner. He ran his hands over the leather upholstery and lacquered walnut door panels. From the back of the front seat, a bar folded down.

"Hey, man, no booze."

The lieutenant apologized with a smile. "It seems to have 'disappeared.' "

"Where d'you think that shooting was?" Lyons asked him.

"In the hills. Perhaps higher on the road."

The dirt lane switchbacked across the mountainside. Overarching pines hid the sky. Rivulets of clear water splashed from rocks above the road, causing areas of mud. Lyons motioned to the lieutenant.

"Stop!"

Ahead of them, the road passed over a gentle hillside. Cleared ground on both sides of the road had once been planted with corn; a few withered stalks still stood. A burned-out house overlooked the road. Bullets had pocked the adobe walls. As the Cadillac slowed to a stop, Gadgets leaned forward. Blancanales scanned the upslope hillsides.

"What do you see?" Gadgets asked Lyons.

"Mines!" the lieutenant shouted as he jammed the shift into reverse.

Several round depressions in the road had filled with water. A shovel lay at the side of the road. As the Cadillac's tires spun backward in the sand and gravel of the road, they saw a man step out of the brush.

He wore dark green fatigues and a beret. A red star on the beret identified him as a guerrilla with the Stalinist Popular Liberation Forces. But the four men in the Cadillac ignored the ideological identification. Their eyes fixed on the weapon he held.

An RPG-7 rocket launcher.

Dropping to one knee, the guy shouldered the launcher. He took his hand off the pistol grip and removed the warhead's safety cap. He cocked the hammer.

The Cadillac shuddered and rocked as it hurtled backward. As if in a nightmare, they all saw the man aiming the rocket at the center of the windshield. Lieutenant Lizco had the accelerator to the floor, but it would not save them.

As the guerrilla's finger pulled the trigger, Lyons grabbed the steering wheel and jerked it toward him. The change in direction gave greater traction to the tires. The Cadillac whipped through a two-wheeled backward turn, the rear end bumping uphill, smashing through bushes and pine saplings.

The rocket shrieked over the hood and into the distance. The explosion came an instant later.

"Forward now!"

With the rocking Cadillac tilted backward up the hillside at forty-five degrees, the lieutenant accelerated. He whipped the steering wheel all the way to his left.

For a sickening instant, the out-of-control Coupe de Ville again balanced on two wheels. Then Gadgets and Blancanales threw themselves against the inside of the rear door to shift the weight of the car. With a crash, the Cadillac fell onto all four wheels and fishtailed across the dirt road.

"And I always thought the rebels liked reporters," Gadgets commented.

"Perhaps they can't read," Blancanales said as he took out his M-16/M-203.

"You remember the expression?" Gadgets asked. He held his CAR-15 and scanned the mountainsides. " 'The pen is mightier than the sword'? I tell you, a rocket puts down any typewriter."

"Where now?" Lyons asked the lieutenant as he took his Atchisson from its case.

"There is another road," the grim-faced man at the wheel replied. "Actually only a trail. Perhaps we will take it. It is beyond the landing strip."

"But the firefight we heard—"

"Yes. That is also beyond the landing strip."

Blancanales leaned forward. "The Commies must have set a one-two ambush. The one up ahead, then that one back there. They hit the army up there, and then if a react-force comes up the road, they hit it too. Or if the unit up there broke out, they'll run into the second ambush on the way down. Standard procedure, straight out of the book."

"What's the book say about our situation?" Lyons asked the ex-Green Beret.

"Said to cover your ass," Blancanales answered.

"Hide out," Gadgets added. "Make them find you. And when they do, ambush them."

"Tough to hide a Cadillac Coupe de Ville," Lyons commented. "Lieutenant, how about we ditch this monster and cut overland?"

"That is also very dangerous. The road comes soon. Let us chance it."

"You're the driver." Lyons buckled on a bandolier of Atchisson magazines. "But I'd rather walk than play tag with RPGs."

"Second the motion," Gadgets told his partners. "When the Ironman says he's afraid, it's time to shake."

"Not afraid," Lyons corrected. He kept his eyes on the hillsides as he spoke. "We just don't have time for this nonsense."

They passed the airstrip. Pushing the overweight luxury car to its limit, the lieutenant continued into the hills. Over the rattling of gravel and rocks in the fenders, they heard no more rifle fire.

"The road comes soon," Lieutenant Lizco stressed. "Very soon. All will be okay."

At one hundred kilometers an hour, the Cadillac lurched across the gravel. A straightaway led over the crest of a low hill.

Bouncing over the top, they drove into the wreckage and death of the ambush.

6

As their hands closed on their weapons, the men of Able Team saw this scene: The road widened. Engineers had graded flat the low slopes of a hill to provide a service area for road maintenance. At the downslope edge of the area, trucks had dumped loads of gravel and broken stone. Pine trunks had been stacked a few meters away. To the north, the road went over a low rise to continue into the mountains.

A steep hillside overlooked the road and service area. High brush and pine saplings had concealed the guerrillas.

The ambush had evidently been quick and efficient. The first truck burned at the far side of the clearing, only ten meters short of the exit to the north. Corpses of soldiers indicated that gunfire had come from the hillside above them and from the rise ahead of the truck. The autofire had driven the survivors back from the truck and into the center of the kill zone.

The second and third trucks had been hit with RPGs as they attempted to back out. More sprawled corpses of soldiers indicated that the guerrillas had closed a circle around the unit. Running from the infernos of the trucks, the soldiers had run into the rifle fire of guerrillas waiting behind the piles of gravel and stacked pines.

Now the guerrillas, wearing workshop-stitched uniforms, tennis shoes and black nylon web-gear, herded captured soldiers through the smoke and flames of the killground. Guerrillas with red stars on their berets stripped uniforms from the living, and from the dying and dead soldiers. Other guerrillas gathered the captured uniforms, weapons and boots.

On the far side of the ambush site, where the road headed north away from Able Team, two jeeps with pedestal-mounted M-60 machine guns parked, the drivers pulling on the handbrakes. A guerrilla officer with an Uzi left the second jeep. Unlike the others in the ragged platoon of mountain fighters, the leader appeared military. Clean-shaven and short-haired, he wore clean fatigues and polished black boots. Guerrillas moved to the jeeps with their loads of captured equipment.

The freedom fighters of the Popular Liberation Forces made no secret of how they would dispose of their prisoners.

Two Communists forced a naked teenage soldier to his knees as a third Communist put a pistol muzzle to the boy's face.

The pistol flashed, the corpse flopped back as the Coupe de Ville hurtled over the rise.

Lyons thumbed his Atchisson's fire-selector to semi-auto. "The one with the Uzi—the officer—we take him alive!"

"Lyons, no!" Blancanales leaned from the back seat. "We can race through! We got the speed—"

A Communist sentry turned at the sound of the onrushing car, the AK-47 he held rising to his shoulder.

Lyons fired. At 1200 feet per second, a spray of steel balls crossed the ten-meter distance to tear through the guerrilla's chest. The other Communists heard the boom of the assault shotgun and whirled as their dead comrades flew back.

A shiny symbol of capitalist decadence hurtled at them. Gadgets's Colt rifle flashed autofire from the back windows, lines of 5.56mm slugs—military hardball alternating with hollowpoints—scythed through groups of bearded, swaggering Communists.

Victory became annihilation as they died with their ComBloc rifles and RPGs slung over their shoulders.

The AKs of the guerrillas guarding the soldiers went on line at the Cadillac. Reprieved from execution, the soldiers started grabbing the weapons, punching the Communists, wrestling them for their AKs.

"Lieutenant!" Blancanales shouted. "Continue! Go through!"

"No!" Lyons countered. "We waste these shits." He sighted on a guerrilla and fired. A single blast of steel killed one Communist and wounded another.

"Use your head! It's not our war—"

"We need those jeeps!" Lyons shouted.

Lieutenant Lizco screamed his words like a battle cry. "We kill them all!"

Flashing past the flames of the second and third trucks, the lieutenant spun the steering wheel hard to the right, aiming for the gap between the first and second trucks. The Cadillac sideslipped, bounced across the road, threw mud and gravel. But it did not quite clear the first truck.

The left rear fender clipped the steel of the troop truck's plate-steel rear bumper. Metal tore. The impact threw Gadgets and Blancanales hard against the rear left door. Lyons fell against the lieutenant.

As the heavy Cadillac raced through mud, Lieutenant Lizco whipped the wheel to the left. Lyons flew toward the passenger-side open window.

Lyons somersaulted out of the Cadillac and slammed into the road, rolling. Stunned, he realized he no longer held his Atchisson. His reflexes took over.

He scrambled on all fours through the acrid smoke of the burning trucks. Clawing the Colt Python from the holster at the small of his back, he pointed the .357 Magnum at a smoke-shrouded form holding an AK.

As his finger tightened on the trigger, he saw a bloody teenager in the uniform of the Salvadoran army. Lyons's thumb caught the hammer at full cock.

"Amigo!" Lyons shouted out one of the few Spanish words he knew.

"*¿Americano?*" The sight of a blond, blue-eyed North American in slacks and sports coat on his hands and knees in the mud amazed the Salvadoran trooper. The youth grabbed the North American's coat and jerked him to his feet.

A guerrilla blundered into them. Lyons fired a 158-grain hollowpoint point-blank into the man's face. As the corpse fell back, Lyons snatched the AK from its grasp.

The AK in his left hand, the Colt Python Magnum in his right, Lyons dashed for the cover of a gravel pile. Beside him, the Salvadoran private grabbed a wounded friend from the ground. The young soldier dragged the wounded boy away. Lyons turned to cover their retreat.

Near the trucks, a guerrilla shouldered an RPG and aimed it at the careering Cadillac. Lyons thumb-cocked his revolver and sighted on the rocketer's head. He squeezed off the shot, saw the hollowpoint throw the man sideways.

The Communist's dead hand triggered the launcher. The rocket's primary charge sent the warhead skittering over the road and into a flaming truck.

Flame and black smoke enveloped the hillside as the RPG's warhead exploded, spraying metal and burning rubber from the already fire-gutted truck.

The sheet of flame churned into the sky. A guerrilla

Kill School

staggered from the flaming brush, his hair and beard burning, his hands and face melted. The flame-blinded Communist wandered in horror for an instant, then fell down the embankment and thrashed with the agony of slow death by shock.

In the Coupe de Ville, the lieutenant whipped the steering wheel from side to side, his foot holding the accelerator to the floor. The car shuddered as the tires spun.

"Carl's out there!" Blancanales shouted to Gadgets.

"That's their problem!" Gadgets yelled back.

A guerrilla saw the Cadillac swerving toward him. Despite the big car's high powered engine, the Cadillac seemed to move in slow motion, the engine roaring but not accelerating the vehicle as its spinning tires sprayed mud and gravel. The guerrilla calculated the path of the Cadillac as he dashed forward. He would fire directly into the open windows of the armored luxury car.

Both Lieutenant Lizco and Gadgets saw the guerrilla sprinting toward the Cadillac, AK flashing. Slugs hammered the steel of the car's fenders and doors. Lieutenant Lizco cranked the steering wheel in the opposite direction. Gadgets pointed his CAR.

The Cadillac careened sideways, the muzzle of the Colt autorifle touching the guerrilla's olive-drab uniform as Gadgets fired a burst.

AK slugs tore the leather seat mere inches behind the lieutenant. Then the mangled fender struck the guerrilla's legs like a sheet-steel ax, severing one leg, impaling the other. The Cadillac dragged the guerrilla over the road, his body tumbling like a tangle of bloody rags.

In a wide, sweeping turn, the lieutenant attempted to circle around the first truck.

The Cadillac left the ground.

What? Gadgets thought as he saw the scene of burn-

ing trucks and running men fall below him. Can this
Cadillac Coupe de Ville fly?

Then the shock and roar answered his unspoken question.

A land mine.

After an instant of flight, the Cadillac hit the road.
Steel-plate armor under the passenger compartment had
saved Gadgets and Blancanales from the mine's blast
and shrapnel, but not the vehicle. Minus the right rear
wheel and fender panel, the Cadillac bounced to a stop.

The lieutenant attempted to continue. As he stood on
the accelerator, the drive shaft, blast twisted and torn
from the differential, flailed at the underside of the
Cadillac like a rotary hammer gone wild.

Numb, disoriented, his vision spinning, Blancanales
smelled gasoline. "Wizard, Lieutenant, out!"

A hand grabbed Blancanales. Gadgets leaned in the
Cadillac and dragged Blancanales clear. Blinking at two
suns, Blancanales realized he lay flat on his back. He
felt his M-16/M-203 in his hands.

Pushing himself up with the butt of the assault rifle-
grenade launcher, Blancanales's double vision saw two
scenes of Gadgets throwing gear and weapons from the
Cadillac while the lieutenant fired Lyons's Atchisson at
guerrillas rushing the blast-wrecked Cadillac.

Slugs tore over Blancanales. Too dizzy to stand or run,
he rolled onto his stomach. He braced his M-16/M-203
on the road and searched for the guerrilla gunner.

A teenager with a red hammer and sickle embroidered
onto his beret rushed from the smoke. Blancanales
sighted on the center of the two spinning images and
pulled the trigger. Nothing. He touched the M-16's receiver. The magazine empty, the bolt had locked back.

His left hand found the trigger assembly of the M-203
grenade launcher. Closing one eye, he fired the grenade

as the teenage Communist sighted his AK on the North Americans.

The 40mm HE fragmentation grenade disintegrated the boy's torso. Like half a marionette, the legs and pelvis danced about in the mud of the road as the dead boy's nerves died.

"Just use bullets, will you?" Gadgets shouted through the chaos. "That's overkill!"

Diving into the mud, Lieutenant Lizco and Gadgets escaped a searing wave of flame from the Cadillac as the spilled gasoline flashed. The fireball rose to join the smoke of the burning trucks and hillside.

Waiting until the heat-flash faded, Gadgets dragged two cases of Able Team equipment away from the Cadillac.

"Ammo!" Blancanales called out.

Lieutenant Lizco, dragging other cases, unslung a bandolier of magazines and tossed it to the North American.

Blancanales tore open a Velcro closure to find a box mag of 12-gauge shells. He slung the bandolier and his M-16/M-203 over his shoulder and pulled out his Beretta 93-R. Staggering to his feet, he searched the ground near the burning Cadillac for weapons and gear.

"We got it all! We got it!" Gadgets shoved Blancanales away from the fire. "Put out rounds!"

"I don't have rounds!"

"Here." Gadgets shrugged the Atchisson off his shoulder. "There's ammo for this monster somewhere—"

"I got it," Blancanales gasped.

AKs banging, three Communists broke from the smoke and flames and sprinted for the parked jeeps. Slugs zipped past Gadgets and Blancanales as the guerrillas sprayed autofire in all directions. Lieutenant Lizco returned the fire with a mud-splashed M-16. All three

ComBloc weapons were pointed at the men staggering away from the burning Cadillac.

Blancanales flipped down the Atchisson's fire-selector and pulled the trigger at the three guerrillas. The assault shotgun roared in full-auto mode.

As he saw the running Communists contort in a mist of sprayed blood, the slamming recoil of the weapon knocked Blancanales backward. Sitting in the mud, he pocketed the empty mag and slapped in another magazine of 12-gauge shells. Before standing again, he glanced at the fire-selector and clicked it up to semiauto.

Across the clearing, Lyons heard the Atchisson booming. He lay behind the cover of the gravel pile and stacked pines with several Salvadoran soldiers, some wounded, others dazed. Teenage soldiers put out aimed shots into the confusion.

Lyons scanned the road and maintenance area for the guerrilla officer. He knew the value of capturing a member of the Communist command cadre. The officer would not only know the locations and patrol routes of guerrilla units, but also—as demonstrated by the efficient and deadly ambush—information on army movements. Perhaps he would have details on the security of Able Team's target, Colonel Quesada.

But black smoke drifted over the road and clearing, hiding the guerrillas and the surviving soldiers. He listened for the 9mm popping of the officer's Uzi. He did not hear the weapon.

Perhaps the officer had already died... or escaped.

Above the road, flames consumed several pines. The green brush burned slowly. Wind came for a moment. Lyons saw a Communist on the hillside leave the smoking brush and take cover in a tangle of low pine branches. A second later, heavy-caliber slugs slammed into the wood sheltering Lyons. The Salvadorans went flat to the ground to escape the downward-directed autofire.

Lyons shifted his position. Aiming his captured AK at the hidden gunman's cover, he sprayed out the magazine of 7.62mm ComBloc slugs. But the wind had shifted and the smoke obscured the hillside again.

He dropped the AK and sprinted for the embankment. Squatting beneath the tangle of pine branches, he waited.

The gunman fired again. Lyons took out his Python and checked the cylinder. He dropped the four unfired cartridges into his pocket. Slapping in a speed-loader, he waited.

Smoke swirled around him as the wind shifted. Clawing up the embankment, he looked into the muzzle of a G-3.

His eyes searching for targets near the burning Cadillac, the guerrilla did not see Lyons's face only two feet in front of him. Lyons put a hollowpoint into the gunman's right ear.

Lyons scrambled over the top of the hill and snaked into the tangle. He stripped the dead man of his bandolier and G-3, then scanned the road for other guerrillas.

Dragging a bullet-shattered leg, a Communist crawled toward the downhill edge of the clearing. Lyons sighted on the man's shoulder and fired. The bullet impacted inches to the guerrilla's right. Lyons corrected for the rifle's misaligned sights and fired again. Instead of hitting the man's shoulder, the bullet struck the guerrilla in the small of the back.

Lyons glanced at the G-3. A small star had been scratched on the plastic stock and then painted in red. On the receiver, the stamp of the army of El Salvador identified the source of the weapon. Years of wear and pitting from corrosion showed on the receiver and metal parts.

He aimed at the head of a dead guerrilla on the far side of the clearing and squeezed off two careful shots. The first slug missed by inches, the second hit the guerrilla in the chest. The old rifle no longer had the accuracy to hit a six-inch-diameter target at one hundred meters.

Lyons resumed his visual search for the officer, but did not spot him. He saw Salvadoran soldiers pulling their dead and wounded away from the burning vehicles. One soldier hacked at the faces of wounded guerrillas with his bayonet.

Beyond the smoking hulks, he heard the Atchisson boom once again. Two troopers threw a Communist guerrilla to the ground and stood on his arms while another soldier searched him.

A Communist appeared from a wall of smoke. He had no rifle. Coming directly up toward Lyons, the teenage guerrilla sprinted for the safety of the hillside. Lyons waited.

As the boy scrambled up the hill, Lyons clubbed him with the ancient G-3. The blow broke off the plastic stock of the German rifle.

Dragging his prisoner by the collar, Lyons joined his partners and Salvadoran allies. They squatted behind the cover of the jeeps, alert to the threat of guerrilla snipers.

Gadgets, wild-eyed with adrenaline, greeted him with jive. "Hey, it's the Ironman. Who's too cool to cruise with his amigos. Did you have a good time? Out here with the Salvos?"

Lyons looked around at the hellground. No officer. Only dead teenagers.

The dead teenagers of the Popular Liberation Forces.

Dead teenagers of the Salvadoran Army.

The ashes and black bones of the anonymous dead near the burned-out trucks.

Lyons took a second to think of an answer to Gadgets's question.

"Next time," he said, "I fasten my safety belt."

7

In the swirling smoke of the burning vehicles and forest, Lieutenant Lizco and his North American allies searched the captured jeeps. They saw that the Popular Liberation Force jeeps still bore the markings of a Salvadoran army unit—Las Boinas Verdes. Both jeeps had army radios. They found thousands of rounds for the M-60 machine guns in foil-sealed U.S. Army ammo boxes. In one jeep, they found clean uniforms and weapons taken from Salvadoran army troops.

"Las Verdes," the lieutenant commented, tapping the stenciled markings on the jeeps. "The Green Berets. They are stationed in Gotera." He pointed to the Salvadoran soldiers. "They are with the same unit."

"Can't be special forces." Lyons looked at the carnage a single platoon of guerrillas had inflicted on the soldiers.

"It is only a name," the lieutenant told him. "Only words. And paint."

"No red stars," Gadgets wondered. "Commie decals on their beanies and rifles, but not on the jeeps. Why?"

"Perhaps they used the jeeps to lure the trucks into the ambush," Blancanales suggested.

"Save the mystery for later." Lyons glanced toward the Salvadoran soldiers. "They've seen us, they know we're North Americans. What now?"

"Tell them we're just hardcore tourists," Gadgets suggested.

"Lieutenant, how long will we be in this area?" Blancanales asked.

"Until the rain comes." The lieutenant looked up at the gathering clouds. "And Quesada comes."

"So we could be here for days, waiting." Lyons watched the teenage Salvadoran soldiers tending their wounded and gathering their dead. "When they get back, everyone in El Salvador will know we're here."

Blancanales considered the problem. "We may be compromised," he said, "but I don't think so. However, we must guard the lieutenant's identity. If they see him, he cannot remain in his country."

"So what's the scheme?" Lyons demanded.

Blancanales looked to Lieutenant Lizco. "How can we explain ourselves? What would those soldiers believe?"

"They would not believe you are tourists," the lieutenant said, laughing. "And they know you are not journalists. Journalists would not help a soldier. We will say you are mercenaries. Traveling through Salvador to Honduras. Yes?"

Gadgets nodded. "On our way to play zap-zap with the Nicos. Makes sense to me."

"They will believe you are professional soldiers," the lieutenant stressed.

"That's what we'll tell them," Lyons agreed.

The lieutenant tore strips of OD green cloth from a captured uniform. "Cover your faces. They will understand."

"Who were those masked men!" Gadgets took a green strip and covered his face.

"Pol, we've got to question those prisoners." Lyons tied a strip over his face. "Wizard, Lieutenant, if you two can dump all this equipment and get us ready to move...."

The Salvadoran soldiers stood around the three surviving guerrillas. They abused the prisoners, taunting
them, kicking their wounds. Some of the soldiers
pointed their rifles at the guerrillas' heads. Crossing
the clearing in a jog, Lyons called out, "No! No
shoot!"

"¡No dispare!" Blancanales shouted in Spanish.

The two North Americans pushed through the group
of Salvadorans. The prisoners lay against the gravel
pile. Flies swarmed on their wounds. One had passed
out from blood loss, his life draining away from
through-and-through buckshot wounds to his legs.
Blancanales quickly slipped out his knife and cut away
the man's pant legs. He used the cloth to make pressure
bandages. The other seriously wounded guerrilla had a
bullet-shattered forearm, but had already bandaged it
himself. The third prisoner, the panicked teenager
Lyons had clubbed with the G-3, stared around at the
soldiers like a trapped animal.

One of the Salvadoran soldiers spoke to Blancanales
in rapid Spanish. Blancanales answered. Then the soldier spoke again with a sneer.

"He asked me why I help the Communists," Blancanales translated for Lyons. "And I told him they'd die
otherwise. He said they're dying no matter what."

The arm-wounded guerrilla spoke to the frightened
boy. The boy crossed himself. The wounded guerrilla
laughed at the Catholic gesture. He raised his clenched
fist in a defiant proletarian salute. Blancanales pushed
the man's arm down and spoke to him quickly. The guy
laughed again.

Lyons stepped forward and put his foot on the man's
good arm. The man shook his head, then glanced
around to the crowd of soldiers to emphasize the point.

"Tell this Commie to go easy on the provocations,"
Lyons told Blancanales. "And tell the soldiers that *we*

took these prisoners. What happens to them is our decision.''

"We don't want to tell them that." Blancanales gave the problem a moment of thought. Then he spoke to the soldiers in careful, evenly spoken words as he examined the shattered arm of the second guerrilla.

The soldiers argued with Blancanales. The loudest soldier stepped forward. His G-3, pointed at the wounded prisoners, boomed twice before Blancanales knocked the weapon aside. Lyons grabbed the rifle and pushed the soldier away.

Holding up his clenched fist one last time, his blood fountaining from his heart, the wounded guerrilla died. The corpse thrashed, and in death it gasped air through the hole in its chest. The other wounded prisoner, the unconscious one, also died, but without spasms.

Lyons threw the G-3 aside and unslung his Atchisson in one motion. His face masked, he faced the Salvadorans with the assault shotgun, the fire-selector on full-auto, his finger on the trigger. He heard movement behind him. "Pol! Watch my back—"

"It's me, it's me," said the lieutenant.

Holding up his knife, Blancanales made eye contact with all the Salvadorans. Then he indicated the wounded boy at his feet and spoke calmly to the soldiers. The soldiers, only moments ago enraged, now laughed.

The lieutenant stepped up behind Lyons and whispered a translation. "He said the guerrilla will pray for a bullet before he dies."

Blancanales slowly leaned to the bloody boy and helped him to his feet. He turned the boy around. While all the soldiers watched, Blancanales tore a tourniquet off a dead guerrilla and tied the boy's hands behind him. Then he shoved the boy toward the jeeps.

"Watch my back, Ironman," Blancanales whispered as he passed. "Those punks are crazy."

Keeping his eyes on the soldiers, Lyons backed up, the muzzle of the Atchisson threatening the group with death by high-velocity steel. The loud-mouthed soldier who had killed the two wounded men spat at Lyons, but the other soldiers grabbed him and restrained him.

Another soldier stepped toward Lyons. Lyons swiveled the autoshotgun to point at the teenager's chest. The soldier put up both hands, palms open. Then he reached up and took off his OD green beret. He held it out to Lyons.

"Muchas gracias por su ayuda, guerrero."

Taking his left hand off the foregrip of the Atchisson, Lyons motioned the young soldier forward. The soldier gave him the beret. Lyons flipped it onto his head. He set it at a rakish angle, like a movie-star hero, as he continued backing away.

Behind him, he heard the engines of the jeeps start. Lyons gave the group of soldiers a left-handed salute. But he did not turn his back.

"Come get me," he called out.

A jeep bumped backward to him. Not taking his eyes from the Salvadorans, Lyons stepped into the jeep. He put his knee in the seat and braced the Atchisson on the backrest.

As Able Team left the kill zone behind, the Salvadoran soldiers waved. The jeeps followed the road over the rise and around a bend. Only then did Lyons click up his Atchisson's safety. His hand-radio buzzed. Lyons set down his weapon and searched through his pockets.

"Wiz-a-rado a-qui," Gadgets jived through the electronic encoding circuits of the NSA equipment. Any counterinsurgent operatives monitoring radio communications would intercept only bursts of static as the en-

crypting circuits of Able Team's hand-radios instantaneously coded and decoded every transmission. "*¿Que pasa?* Gonna do any more favors for people?"

"Favors for who?" Lyons watched the forested hillsides above the road as he spoke into his hand-radio. "That Commie? Fighting is one thing, but torturing and murdering fifteen-year-olds is something else."

"Hey, man," Gadgets's voice responded with a laugh. "Ricardo and me are already buddies. I meant those Salvos back there—first we save them, then they want to off us."

"I didn't do anything for them," Lyons answered. "We needed these jeeps. Ricardo's the kid's name?"

"Yeah," replied Gadgets's voice. "And he is fifteen. Jesus, I been here three hours and the Pol said it straight last night. 'Salvador is the asshole of the world.' I want to go home, where teenagers smoke grass and screw their teenybop girlfriends. This scene down here is *heavy*."

"Do your job, Wizard," muttered Lyons. "Sooner you do it, sooner we go back."

"I'm doing my job. Have you checked out the radios in these jeeps? Ask the lieutenant to look at the frequencies."

Lyons looked over to the lieutenant. He had heard everything Gadgets Schwarz said over the hand-radio. He clenched his jaw with anger. He pointed to the dial of the jeep's radio console.

"That radio. That number is the frequency of the Boinas Verdes. That is the frequency of the army's helicopters. That radio. I do not know about the other radio. I have never seen it before."

After Lyons relayed the information, Gadgets asked, "What other radio?"

"There's another set here. Looks like a civilian unit.

No brand name, no model names or numbers. Only numbers on the dials. A black radio, with a dial and a microphone. Nothing else."

"Stand by to stop," Gadgets told Lyons. "I want to check out that black box. Maybe we could monitor Commie frequencies. The Pol will pull when he sees good cover."

Unable to contain his anger, Lieutenant Lizco spoke suddenly. "To slander my country is easy. We have many troubles. The hatred and the violence of four hundred years make the politics of my country insane. But hear me, *norteamericano*. Your country makes it worse. One president talks of human rights and the next president talks of making war to make peace. But it is all only noise for the television—"

"Don't talk that shit to me." Lyons's talents did not include courtesy or diplomatic explanations of United States foreign policy. "This place is a hellhole of Nazis and psychos. You going to blame the massacre in 1932 on the United States? Did the U.S. bring in the death squads? Can't tell me that—"

The lieutenant cut him off. "I can tell you this. In October 1979, the army took the government away from the generals and the families. My brother and father worked with the Junta, they told me all this. The army created the land reforms. The army sent the corrupt generals and colonels into exile. The army disbanded Orden. The army fought the Communists.

"There were only two thousand or three thousand guerrillas in the mountains," he continued, "not all of them Communists. The Junta hoped the reforms and the justice and human rights would win the war. We hoped the United States would lend us the money to make the reforms. We hoped for weapons to fight the Communists.

"Nothing came from the great democracy in the north. No money, no rifles, no helicopters, nothing. Only politicians and journalists.

"The dreamers and idealists in the Junta promised change. But they had no money for the people, no weapons for the army.

"The idealists could not stop the counterrevolution. They could not stop the death squads. The national guard, the national police, the Orden—they murdered thousands. The families destroyed the Junta.

"To please the new administration in the north, the families formed the Second Junta, the Gang of Death. The gang also promised reforms, but what they gave the people was murder. The gang ruled by the bullet and the machete.

"When the gang stopped the reforms, then it was that your new president sent help. Hundreds of millions of dollars, rifles, helicopters, Special Forces to train our soldiers to find the idealists and campesinos and teachers hiding in the mountains. Now there are ten thousand guerrillas. Now the guerrillas have the mountains and the roads and the villages—"

"Shut up!" Lyons shouted the lieutenant down. "None of that's my problem. That's your problem. You don't like what your government does, why are you in the army?"

"Someone must fight the Communists," the lieutenant seethed. "And after I defeat them, I will fight the others. And soon enough there will be a new American president. Every time you change presidents, it is as if the United States is another country. There may be hope for El Salvador."

Ahead of them, Blancanales swerved off the dirt road. The lieutenant followed the first jeep. Overhanging trees shadowed a fold in the hillsides. No helicopter or patrol could spot the group.

Blancanales left the front jeep. He walked back to the lieutenant. As he spoke quietly with the Salvadoran, he gave Lyons a glance and a shake of his head. Blancanales and the Salvadoran army officer, their weapons in their hands, went to stand sentry at the turn-off. Gadgets explained to Lyons, "We heard it all, man. I turn on that minimike, and what do I hear? The Ironman alienating our liaison."

"I couldn't let him talk that shit without talking back."

"Why not? Can a word make you bleed? Let him unload his lip on you. Let him talk his Yanqui Go Home routine. You want to debate the history of presidential foreign policy? Or do you want to get Quesada? You don't even read the newspapers, how can you talk about anything?"

"It's what *you* said that started him off."

"Forget it. Let the Pol do the talking." Gadgets glanced to Blancanales, who talked earnestly with the young Salvadoran officer ten meters away. "He's got the talent for it. Why don't you watch the teenager? He's been praying nonstop. I got to check out this funky radio here."

Gadgets spread out tools and electronics on the seats of the jeep. Lyons went to the other jeep. The boy lay in the back, tied hand and foot, his head pillowed on OD green cans of belted 7.62mm NATO.

"Hey, Ricardo. How you doing?"

The boy looked up with tears and blood streaming down his face. *"Señor comandante, por favor. Tengo quinze años. No soy un comunista. No soy un comunista...."*

Lyons glanced at the clotted blood matting the boy's

hair. He went to the cases of gear and searched through the equipment for the first-aid kit. With alcohol and a wad of tissue, Lyons cleaned the clots away from the cut on the boy's head. The care indicated to the teenager that the hard-eyed North American did not intend to execute him.

"Gracias, señor. Gracias—"

"Be quiet, kid. Everything'll be okay. If you'll quit the People's Army of Murder, I'll take you to L.A. We got a half million Salvadorans up there already."

"Okay, *señor*. Okay, okay."

"Okay, what?"

"Okay, okay. *Solamente quinze, años, no soy un soldado....*"

Lyons called out to Blancanales. "Hey, Pol. What did this kid tell you?"

Jogging over to Lyons, Blancanales answered in a low voice. "No time to question him yet. You going to bandage his head? Good. Excellent interrogation technique, gaining the confidence and gratitude of a prisoner. I wouldn't have expected it of you."

"Because I'm just an animal, right?" Lyons shot back, angry at his partner. "I don't let junior hotshots badmouth my country and my president, so I'm an animal. I guess I'll just go clean my weapon. Get ready to annihilate another group of Latin American intellectuals and social reformers. Onward Yanqui soldiers...."

A voice blared out. Lyons and Blancanales whipped around to see Gadgets switching on a tape recorder. He set the recorder in front of the unmarked, nonmilitary radio.

Joining his partners, he said, "That voice sounds official. Like he's a commander. Maybe you could fake an answer to throw the Commies off us."

"Perhaps...." Blancanales moved quickly to the jeep. He listened to the transmission.

"It's ComBloc equipment?" Lyons asked.

Gadgets shook his head. "This is good equipment. The black box comes with encoding and screech transmission circuits. It's as good as what we got from the National Security Agency. Even has a digital code switch. If you don't know the code, you can't turn it on."

"How'd *you* do it?"

"Bypassed the ten-key with my pulse generator. The electronics put infinite combinations into the circuit until it clicked."

Lieutenant Lizco left his sentry position at the road. He returned to the jeep and listened carefully to the voice, concentrating on the voice itself and its speech patterns. He slowly looked up to the North Americans, his face slack with disbelief.

"That," he said, "is Quesada...."

8

In the army *cuartel* of San Francisco Gotera, North American and European journalists crowded around the commander of Las Boinas Verdes, Colonel Alfredo Perez, as he spoke in English of the U.S.-sponsored pacification program. He posed against a ceiba tree, his camouflage fatigues starched and creased, his jump wings flashing on his chest, an Uzi machine pistol slung casually over his right shoulder. His deep, resonant voice boomed in the garrison courtyard.

At one time, the cobblestoned courtyard—brilliant with bougainvillea and hibiscus, shaded by the ceiba—echoed with typing and ringing telephones as the town officials of Gotera administered the prosperous farming region. Secretaries hurried from office to office in the two-story stucco-and-tile buildings framing the courtyard. The national police maintained an office on the ground floor where officers slept through their careers.

A guerrilla bomb had destroyed the national-police office. The soldiers now quartered in the civic buildings had placed a Browning Model 1919A6 .30-caliber machine gun pointing out through a window bricked-in to a horizontal slit. The weapon's field of fire included the town square, the Cine Morazan, the church, and a café advertising Coca-Cola and Cervezas Pilsner. Where the now-deceased policemen had slept with their chairs tilted against the walls, soldiers slept against sandbags. On the second-floor balconies where secretaries had minced from office to office in their tight skirts, their heels clicking on the tiles, soldiers played cards behind rows of sandbags, oblivious to the American-accented English of their commander.

"The political details and legal technicalities don't concern me. My duty is the protection of the administrators and the campesinos. If the guerrillas kill the government workers or the farmers who work the land, they kill the reforms.

"Though the war requires more supplies of material from the United States, the reforms are the best weapon we have to defeat the Communists.

"While the Marxists promise a new social order, the government of El Salvador creates a new order.

"The guerrillas make promises while they burn fields and cut roads and destroy bridges. We issue land titles and loan money for seed and fertilizer.

"We'll win. It may take a year or two to drive all the Communists back to Nicaragua and Cuba and Russia, but we'll win because the people of El Salvador are with us."

Two of the colonel's aides applauded his speech. The journalists glanced at their watches, bored. Expecting the newsmen to snap photos, the colonel turned his profile to the group. But no shutters clicked. The colonel dropped his pose and leaned against the ceiba tree.

"Questions?" he asked the journalists.

A gray-haired reporter in a *guayabera* shirt and plaid Bermuda shorts held up a hand. He held a cassette recorder to tape the colonel's answer.

"Colonel Perez, this morning I saw two bodies just outside town here. Two middle-aged men. Looked poor, had callused hands like farmers—"

"Yes, it is terrible. The terrorists always take the good men, the men who work for a living. If the farmers refuse the propaganda of the Communist terrorists, they're shot like dogs. Next question.''

"Colonel Perez, allow me to finish, please. One had this piece of paper wadded in his mouth." The gray-haired reporter held up a sheet of thin, yellowish paper with printed and typed text. "This land title granted the man ownership of seventeen acres of undeveloped land just north of here. I checked it on the map and it's property claimed by the Quesadas. What—''

"What is your question?'' one of the aides demanded. His right hand gripped the flap of his .45 automatic's holster.

"Please state your question, sir,'' the colonel requested.

"What would the Communists have to gain by protecting the Quesadas' property?''

The colonel laughed. "I don't know. I haven't studied Marx. Maybe you should ask the Communists.''

"Have you questioned the Quesadas about the murders?''

"What murders? Next question.''

Another reporter spoke. "Has the tempo of the fighting decreased since the negotiations began?''

"What negotiations? How can a democracy bargain with terrorists? There are no negotiations that I know of... perhaps the leftists and Communist sympathizers have initiated a sham...."

A soldier ran through the dust and the shadows to hand his commander a slip of paper. The colonel glanced at the message. He turned to the journalists.

"Thank you for your attention and concern, gentlemen. I must end the press conference now. *Buenas tardes.*''

One of the newsmen's drivers rushed through the gates of the *cuartel*. He whispered to the journalists.

"Ambush on road. To the north. I hear army radio. We go?"

"Fighting going on?" a photographer asked.

"All over. No danger. Many dead. Soldiers going in trucks."

"Who won?" a writer asked in English, then repeated in Spanish when the Salvadoran driver did not immediately answer. "*¿Quién son los ganadores?*"

The Salvadoran laughed, spoke in English as before. "Mister, who knows? We go see? Yes? We wait for soldiers to go, we follow."

The group moved for the press vans, all of the journalists and photographers speaking to one another. The gray-haired journalist who had questioned the colonel on the murdered campesinos, Alex Johnson of the *San Francisco Globe*, glanced around the *pueblo* square.

In front of the Cine Morazan, he saw a young man speak with the soldiers quartered in the abandoned theater. The young man looked at the group of journalists leaving the *cuartel*, gave the soldiers a salute and crossed the unpaved square to the vans.

The journalists knew the young man as José Lopez, a United States citizen born in Puerto Rico and working with American journalists in Latin America. He spoke excellent English and idiomatic Spanish. Twenty-two years old, a mulatto with wavy close-cut hair, his skin a café au lait that matched the color of most Salvadorans, José had already proved himself invaluable to the North Americans and Europeans. Local people stared at the foreign journalists. José went unnoticed. Salvadorans turned their backs to the questions of the foreigners. José gossiped and joked with campesinos and soldiers and village women.

The young man went to Alex Johnson. As the other reporters crowded into the vans, José whispered a report to the San Francisco journalist.

"This commander's a complete fuck-up. He's lost a hundred men in the past three months. Not prisoners and wounded. Dead. They're up against the Popular Liberation Forces. The PLF don't take prisoners. The commander only goes through the motions. He resupplies the garrison in Perquin by truck. Which means the guerrillas hit them at their convenience. Maybe once a week there's an ambush like the one the Commies just did. The soldiers are scared shitless."

"What about the two dead farmers?"

"They bury people every morning. Those two today. Three yesterday. One the day before. Every day."

"Who's doing it?"

"Isn't those guys. They don't leave town day or night."

"The Quesadas?"

"They can't say—"

"Won't say?"

"Don't know. If they knew, they'd say. Because the people hate, I mean they *hate*, the Quesada militia. The Quesadas have got helicopters to patrol their property while the soldiers ride around in trucks and get shit on by any Commie with a rifle and a bottle of gasoline. And Mr. Johnson, it is my recommendation that you stay in town. Forget this little press jaunt up to the killing ground."

"Why?"

"Man, because it's unsafe!" José laughed. He pointed to the words whitewashed on the sides of the vans: *Periodistas*, U.S.A., U.K., Alemania. "That paint don't mean a thing when you got a world of bad things happening in those mountains. Besides, there's a unit called the Black Berets coming in off a patrol. They're hardcore LRRPS," he added, referring to their Long Range Reconnaissance Patrols. "They'll be hanging out at the café while they wait for a helicopter out. Those guys will have some information."

"Will they talk to us?"

"You make friends with them. I'm leaving with these hacks."

"Into the mountains? You said—"

"I'm getting out at Lolotiquillo and hiking across to the Quesada plantation for a look-see. I'm meeting a group of friends out there."

Johnson paled at what his assistant told him. "What are you talking about!"

"It's cool. I arranged it in Mexico City. I'll be back in San Salvador in three days."

The older journalist glanced around. The other newsmen waited in the vans. Across the square, soldiers climbed into two troop carriers. A jeep with two pedestal-mounted M-60 machine guns would provide additional firepower on the road.

No one stood so close that Johnson could be overheard. He whispered to his assistant, "Floyd, there's a limit to what you can do."

"Yeah, I hear that. I hear that from the FBI, the Justice Department, the embassy. But if you knew.... If you.... You must understand that I've already gone past the limits. It's the only way to work. I learned that from experts. Specialists in the outer limits."

The troop trucks roared into gear. In the clouding dust, "José Lopez" climbed into a press van. Johnson saw the young man pull a backpack from under the seat. As the van followed the trucks, José leaned forward to speak with the driver.

Alex Johnson stood alone in the dusty town square of San Francisco Gotera, Morazan.

9

"The kid's a murderer," Blancanales reported to his partners after interrogating the teenage guerrilla. "But he isn't a terrorist. Or a Communist."

Able Team crouched near the turn-off from the road. Lyons had carefully whisked away the tire marks of the captured jeeps. Now, from the cover of the brush and saplings that hid the narrow fold in the hillsides, they watched the dirt road and the storm-graying sky for patrols.

Soldiers passing in a truck would not spot the North Americans. The overhead cover of pines screened the jeeps from helicopter observation. Unless an army or guerrilla patrol searched every forested hillside and gully, the patrol would see only one more hillside of tangled brush.

Brilliant afternoon light alternated with cool shadow as storm clouds gathered. A wall of black thunderheads approached from the west. Above the North Americans, patterns of clouds allowed the tropical sun to flash through from time to time, the sunlight searing the cool high-altitude air.

Behind his black lensed sunglasses, Lyons's eyes scanned the road, the hillsides, the panorama of mountains and forest. Blancanales waited for Lyons to comment on the captured boy. He watched the patterns of reflections on Lyons's sunglasses sliding over the black mirrors of the lenses. Lyons held the Atchisson, a round in the chamber and his thumb on the fire-selector. Flies wandered from the autoshotgun's steel to the drops of blood specking his hands. After the wild firefight with the guerrillas, Lyons had cleaned his weapons of residues and blood, but not his hands. He did not flick away the flies.

Blancanales considered how to present the information on the teenager. Could the fifteen-year-old guerrilla hope for mercy from the silent, brooding executioner that Carl Lyons had become? Finally Gadgets broke the silence.

"So what's his story?"

"He isn't political. His sister had a boyfriend who went to fight in the mountains. A neighbor said he'd tell the police about her guerrilla boyfriend if she didn't sleep with him. So Ricardo killed the man with a shovel. People saw him burying the body. Ricardo's family and his sister went to a camp near the coast. But the boy couldn't risk the checkpoints and police, so he had to go to the mountains."

"If it's nothing political," Gadgets asked, "why did he go to the Reds?"

"He didn't. They got him. It's called 'forced recruitment.'"

"What's all that got to do with us?" Lyons finally spoke. "Did he answer the questions or not?"

"He cooperated. Told me what he knew. Though it wasn't much."

"You believe him?" Gadgets asked Blancanales.

"Lying to us is not his number-one concern. He knows we're not official. We would've already killed him. All he wants is transportation to where there's no war."

"Doesn't want to fight for the revolution?" Gadgets asked. "Wait till the *New York Times* hears that."

Blancanales laughed bitterly. "The PLF's number-one assignment here is murdering farmers who buy their land. It's considered an anti-Soviet crime. The boy just wants to get away."

Gadgets turned to Lyons. "You got a problem with turning the kid loose, Ironman? You an ex-PD and him a fugitive from justice?"

Lyons's scans continued, only his lips moving as his eyes searched the distance. "To protect his sister, he killed a lowlife? First Salvadoran I've met who's murdered for a reason. Kid deserves a Nobel Peace Prize. What'd he say about the Reds?"

"We wiped out the hardcore unit. There are more guerrillas to the north, but if we double back, we're in the clear. Except for the army patrols. They stay on the roads. But the Quesadas' militia has helicopters and planes."

"Come sundown," Lyons looked to the west, to the onrushing storm front, "they'll need boats. You get names?"

"Lieutenant Lizco," Blancanales said, glancing to the jeeps where the Salvadoran commando monitored the radios, "doesn't know who it was that Quesada called on the radio. He doesn't know anything about the Verdes. But he said it's entirely possible that Quesada has bought the local army officers."

"You get names from the kid?" Lyons asked.

"Only a nickname. His leader's name is La Víbora, the Snake. He never knew the name of the regional commander. They talked about *el comandante*, but no names."

"And who was it that Quesada called?" Lyons continued.

Gadgets laughed. "Wow! Is that paranoia? The Ironman thinks *el numero uno nazado* works with the Reds?"

"Why not?"

Blancanales corrected Gadgets. "You mean Quesada? The Spanish word's 'Nazi,' just like English."

"I don't care. It rhymes, it's got rhythm. *Sol-da-do, na-za-do. El numero uno soldado nazado.* That's Quesada. But a Nazi running a Commie kill squad? *Extremo dien cai dau loco!*"

Blancanales rocked back on his heels, amazed at Gadgets's linguistic butchery; he had chopped and distorted three European languages plus Vietnamese.

"It's not my conspiracy," Lyons replied. "We should talk to Quesada about it. Storm's coming. I say we move when it hits."

Gadgets shook his head no. "The lieutenant said the grab is set up for El Nazado on the road. We could be waiting for days, a week, he said."

"We don't have to wait a week," Lyons countered. "We know where he is."

"Oh, oh, the man's got a plan." Gadgets sighed. "You want to crash the plantation and take him?"

"Don't want to spend the next month in these mountains. . . ."

Gadgets got to his feet. "Great! Let's go. Get it done! Let's get out of here. I want to go home."

Blancanales looked directly into the black mirrors of Lyons's eyes. "What about the boy?"

"We take him with us." Then Lyons lay down in the brush that concealed them.

"Why you getting comfortable?" Gadgets asked him. "Thought you wanted to move."

Lyons pointed to the storm coming from the sunset. "When it's raining, when it's dark. . .then."

In the silence of the hillside gully, they heard the sudden voice of Quesada speak again from the black radio. Blancanales and Gadgets rushed over to the jeep. Gadgets checked the voice-activated recorder. Blancanales listened as the fascist issued an order. A voice confirmed the instructions. Lieutenant Lizco unfolded a map and found the coordinates.

As they listened to the voices, the lieutenant showed Blancanales the map. He pointed to where they hid at that moment, then to the coordinates given by Quesada.

"The reporters will be killed here," he indicated, "as they return to Gotera."

Calculating the distances, Blancanales nodded.

"What's going on?" Gadgets whispered.

Blancanales held up a hand for patience. He waited until the transmissions between Quesada and the unknown voice ended.

"Whoever his men are," Blancanales told his partner, "soldiers or militia or death squad, they're talking assassination. There's two trucks full of reporters wandering around in the mountains, and Quesada wants them hit."

"Looking for news? They'll be it."

Blancanales turned to the lieutenant. "How can we warn them?"

"If the *periodistas* have a radio.... But if we warn them, perhaps the others—" the lieutenant touched the black radio "—will hear."

Gadgets nodded. "Los Nazados most definitely got the cash for scanners. We warn the press corps, we warn the death corps."

Looking at his watch, then at the gathering storm, Blancanales considered the problem. He took the map to Lyons. He briefed Lyons quickly on the ambush. Pointing to the map, he explained, "We're here, the ambush on the soldiers was here, the ambush on the journalists will be here. Approximately where we ran into that secondary ambush. Quesada said the army will allow the journalists to follow them. Then the army will order them out of the area. They'll be coming back after dark. That's when they get hit. They're coming up into the mountains now. Gadgets doesn't want to risk warning them by radio. He thinks Quesada could have scanners monitoring the journalists' frequency."

Lyons, sitting up, studied the map. He glanced at the sky. "Can't move the jeeps until the storm comes. Need the storm to cover our movement."

"I want to try it, Carl," Blancanales told his partner. "Quesada will present this as a guerrilla atrocity. It could polarize public opinion in the United States and Europe against the liberals and progressives in El Salvador. It might kill the last chance for a negotiated peace."

The black lenses of the sunglasses turned to the mountain above Able Team's concealed position. Lyons pushed his sunglasses above his forehead, California style. He squinted through the pines to study the slopes. He pointed uphill.

"Ambush is on the other side of that mountain. We can't take the jeeps, so we'll hike." Lyons got to his feet. "Ready to go?"

"And the jeeps?"

"They stay here."

"Can't risk that. All our equipment's—"

"Then you and me go. Leave Gadgets here to watch the lieutenant and the boy. We pop the Nazis, signal the Wizard, they bring the jeeps. Or we hike back with the prisoners."

"Prisoners? We don't need to fight the death squad. Only to warn the journalists."

"Fuck the journalists. We want Quesada. If we take the leader of that squad, we're on our way to Quesada."

"Two of us? In unfamiliar territory? Against a death squad?"

Lyons yawned. "Two Americans against ten or twenty Salvladoran Nazis? We got them outnumbered." Looking up at the forested mountains, Lyons reconsidered his bravado. "Three of us. We need a guide."

Crossing to the jeeps, Lyons pulled a knife from his bandolier. Ricardo, sitting in the back of a jeep with plastic handcuffs on his wrists and ankles, saw the North American approach with the knife. His mouth opened to scream.

"It's okay, kid," Lyons told him as he cut the plastic loops. "It's okay. You're taking us sightseeing."

10

Rain hit like breaking waves. Lightning flashes made the black sky white. Winds roared over the forested ridgeline of the mountain. To the west, moments of sundown-red appeared and disappeared in the swirling black clouds.

Following the forms of Ricardo and Blancanales through the semidarkness, Lyons squinted into the storm. Pine branches lashed at his face, the winds swaying the trees around him. They had not yet reached the crest of the mountain. Already, a thousand streams swept mud and forest debris down the steep slope.

Lyons did not want a firefight with the death squad waiting in ambush for the journalists. But he went prepared to kill. He carried the Atchisson, his modified-for-silence Colt Government Model, and his Colt Python. A bandolier of 12-gauge magazines crossed his chest. In the pockets of his black fatigues, he carried grenades and pistol ammunition. Every step taxed his strength, the weight of the weapons driving his boots into the mud.

Lyons calculated they would reach the other side of the mountain after nightfall. Ricardo guided them along the trails switchbacking up the mountain. The teenager had hunted in these mountains with his father. With the guerrillas, the young man had crisscrossed the area in the fight against "class enemies." Now, as the last light of day faded from the storm clouds, Ricardo led two

North American soldiers against Salvadoran fascist assassins. For the reward of an airline ticket and a U.S. visa.

Lyons almost laughed at the irony. This morning, Ricardo had been a "Soviet-sponsored Communist insurgent," representing "a threat to Central American security" and "the peace of the hemisphere." Tonight, the teenager hoped for a ticket out of the war.

Ricardo had talked with Blancanales about the trade schools in the barrios of Los Angeles. Lyons still distrusted Lieutenant Lizco, but he knew he could trust Ricardo with his life. Lyons and Blancanales held the key to the boy's dreams. For the promise of a new life, they had his loyalty.

Would that be a way to end Salvador's tragedy? Give all the teenagers tickets to the United States? Let the Communists and fascists fight it out? Let the politicians die for their country?

Never happen, Lyons told himself. Dreams, fantasies, impossible. Politicians talk for their country, politicians ride in limousines for their country, politicians get rich for their country. But teenagers do the dying.

Put your mind on the mission. And maybe teenagers from Los Angeles and Kansas City and Atlanta won't get the glory of dying for El Salvador.

If the action went as Lyons planned, he and Blancanales would warn the journalists, then take a prisoner. They knew where the Quesadas' militiamen waited. Able Team had seen the area earlier in the day when the guerrillas attempted to ambush the Cadillac there. That piece of luck contributed to the odds of success without a firefight.

The storm slowed them now, but later, after they reached the death squad that waited in ambush, the storm would conceal them as they infiltrated the death squad's position.

If they could take the leader silently, the storm could also cover their retreat with the prisoner. The storm would confuse and frustrate the efforts of the fascists to find their "disappeared" officer.

If they took the leader of the death squad—army officer, fascist militiaman, whoever—he would be the link to Quesada.

If. . . .

First, they must warn the journalists. Blancanales had demanded that. To Lyons, the survival of the journalists meant nothing.

Those vampires, Lyons cursed. Jet-setting the world to exploit suffering and dying. Find someone bleeding, take a picture, send it to New York. The editors write the story. Doesn't matter who dies because of the lies. Doesn't matter if their propaganda screws a country's future.

How often did a journalist spend more than an hour at the scene? Get off the jet, study the situation through the viewfinder of a videocamera, send the tape to New York. Edit five videotapes together, put a giggly blonde and a somber father figure on screen to mouth cue-card lines and the network sold three minutes of commercial time.

Need great video to sell cars and soap and designer jeans. Go to Lebanon, find a street of dead children. Ms Blondie Prime-time talks about the irresponsibility of Israeli defense policy.

Send a crew to El Salvador, do a slow pan of the morgue. Father Network pronounces the latest body-count numbers. The numbers tell the story. Four hundred years of racial and class war explained between shampoo and hemorrhoids.

Got a story that takes a week to tell? Cut it down to thirty-five seconds of screen time. Film at eleven.

Lyons had considered the expediency of allowing the trucks transporting the newsmen and cameramen to trigger the ambush. The muzzle-flashes of the death squad's rifles would reveal their positions.

Maybe the press corps could document their annihilation on camera. Whip out the tape recorders. Zoom in on the bullet-shattered skull. Get those screams on tape. Record the sound of slugs slamming flesh. Catch the sound of a sucking chest wound. A slow pan of the sprawled bodies. Then make notes for the oh-so-somber commentary on the terrible incident. Ten seconds of philosophy and regret formatted for a cue card, then instant replay!

Blancanales had refused. Even if they lost the chance to grab the leader of the death squad, Blancanales considered warning the journalists a moral imperative.

What moral imperatives? What morals? After what he had seen and done, Lyons wondered why the word existed. A word for an unreal concept. After what he'd seen....

That's what he had said that last morning of Flor's life, that last time with her. In a motel bed in Malibu, only hours before she had died in the desert, her body reduced to ash and scorched bones, the last morning of laughter and touching and love....

"It's what you see," he had told her. "After that, dying, thinking about dying isn't the same. You recognize the advantages of being dead. No memories. No thinking...."

He'd said it only hours before she'd died—died because of his bravado and macho stupidity—

"Lyons!"

Blancanales gripped his shoulder. Shaking him, Blancanales whispered through the noise of the wind and beating rain, "You hurt? What happened?"

"What?"

"You made a noise, you groaned. What's wrong?"

"Nothing's wrong. I'm great. I'm a killing machine. Lead the way. Dead meat is my business."

In the faint light, Blancanales studied Lyons's face for a moment. Then he turned and continued uphill, a shadow moving through the shadows of the trees.

Lyons followed. He concentrated on the warm rain washing over his face and body. He touched the rough bark of the trees. He felt the ooze in his boots. He thought of the mission, only the mission.

Quesada.

11

As he stepped from his apartment, Colonel Robert Quesada turned back and promised the two French whores, *"Je reviens tout de suite."*

"Ah, oui, mon général," begged the women. *"Vite. Vite. Il est isolé ici."*

Quesada followed the veranda around the building. Rain poured from the roof in a curtain of water. He stayed close to the building to prevent the splattering streams from spotting his slacks and polo shirt.

In the garden, water covered the cobblestones of the walkway. Wind tore the silk trees and bougainvillea. The gusts created shifting patterns of color and shadow as the birds of paradise and orchids and *copas de oro* swayed in the decorative floodlights.

His Cuban heels clicking across Spanish-patterned tiles, Quesada followed the shelter of the verandas to the wrought-iron gate. Leaning into the storm, he washed his face with rain. He gulped a mouthful. He sloshed the water around in his mouth to wash away the brandy and the taste of the whores' perfumes.

The call from his militia commander had interrupted an afternoon and evening of pleasure. With Señora Quesada and the children remaining in the Colonia San Benito mansion, the colonel had allowed himself the luxury of the young Frenchwomen during his stay at his family's estate. Soon, he would continue on to La Escuela.

At "The School," military discipline ruled. Regulations denied diversions for the soldiers until they completed their course of instruction. The officers and staff enjoyed the pleasures and entertainment of Miami, Las Vegas and Washington, D.C. Sometimes Quesada arranged for his South American friends to enjoy a night of comforts at his *finca*, only minutes from the installation by plane or helicopter. Though he reserved the two Frenchwomen for himself, Miami and Cancun furnished pale-skinned blondes and redheads—with their soft, pouting lips and crème-smooth yet disco-muscled thighs—for the Argentines and Chileans and exiled Bolivians in the guest rooms and beds of the Quesada *finca*.

If the storm had not swept in from the Pacific this afternoon, his superiors in the International Alliance would have expected him to continue on to La Escuela. Though his pilots had assured him the helicopter could make the thirty-minute flight to Reitoca in safety, he enjoyed the excuse of the weather delay. Meetings and planning sessions did not thrill him like the two young blondes. He would fulfill his duty to the International Alliance when the weather cleared.

This detail tonight would deny him the pleasures of the two Paris girls for only a few minutes.

Turning his back on the garden, he stepped to the security entry. His magnetically encoded identity card opened the steel gate.

As the electric motor whirred to roll the gate across, a hard-eyed young soldier glanced through the bulletproof glass of the guard post. He gave his colonel a sharp salute. Returning the salute, Quesada followed the walkway to the family offices.

Mendez waited with a report. A militia lieutenant feared for his pitiless violence, Mendez stood five foot six and weighed two hundred fifty pounds. The man's fat hid iron muscles. His smiling moon face hid the sadism of an inquisitor. Quesada had seen Mendez thumb out the eyes of a boy who would not betray his father.

Rainwater drained from the gray Finca de Quesada uniform that Mendez wore. Mud stained the man's pants up to and above the knee. In the hours since Quesada received the report of the foreigners in the Cadillac attacking the Popular Front Forces, Mendez had visited the roadside villages and isolated farmers in the area. If a shopkeeper or campesino or shepherd had seen the foreigners, they would tell Mendez.

"This is information on the foreigners?" Quesada asked.

"Yes, *padron*. I went to many places, questioned many people. They spoke only of a plane."

"When?"

"Today. Early in the afternoon," replied Mendez. "Down and then gone. But the colonel of Las Boinas Verdes radioed with much more. The foreigners talked with the soldiers. They said they were North American mercenaries traveling to Honduras to fight."

"To Honduras?"

"Yes. They told the soldiers Honduras."

"You have descriptions?"

"One, blond, blue eyes, tall. Another, darker, but also Anglo. The third, a North American who spoke Spanish. Graying hair, perhaps a Puerto Rican. There was a fourth. The soldiers think he is Indian. He did not speak to the soldiers. They all covered their faces."

Quesada considered the information. Four foreign soldiers en route to Honduras. But if they went to fight the Sandinistas, why did they travel through Morazan? *Contras* coming from Texas, Miami and New York flew to Tegucigulpa by jet, then took small planes to El Paraiso. From there, trucks took them to the war.

Could the foreign mercenaries be traveling to La Escuela? Quesada would radio the *comandante* with the descriptions. Perhaps, through some incredible error or breach of security, they had intended to come to the *finca*.

Impossible. No officer at the school would give a recruit or hired instructor the location of the *finca* landing strip. That would risk betrayal of Quesada and risk the secrecy of La Escuela.

No, that could not be the answer. The question of the foreigners' identities and purpose might never be answered. But if they remained in the area, or traveled on through Morazan, Mendez or one of the other men Quesada employed would receive the information. Then Mendez would question the foreigners.

"Colonel!" The radio operator called out from the other office. "A message on the Yankee radio."

Quesada went to the communications room. The radio operator left the colonel alone to review the transmission.

Friends in Washington had supplied Quesada with several radios. Circuitry designed by the electronic engineers of the United States National Security Agency assured secret and secure communications between the *finca* and San Salvador and between Quesada and his fighting units in the mountains.

Now a light glowed on one of the sophisticated consoles, indicating that the radio had received and automatically recorded a coded "burst" transmission. Quesada slipped on the headphones and listened. An electronically detoned voice droned the message.

"Sources in the capital report dispatch of three

American paramilitary operatives to Salvador. Salvadoran national will assist operatives in mission to kidnap you with intent to return you to United States.''

Quesada went cold. Despite the warmth of the humid, stormy night, he shivered as fear and rage seized him.

His friends in Washington had saved him again. The first time, they had ordered the Federal Bureau of Investigation to delay an arrest warrant. The delay allowed him to escape Miami for Salvador.

But now the North American death squad that had annihilated his soldiers in San Francisco and Los Angeles, who had driven him from the sanctuary of his Miami mansion, now that death squad pursued him to Morazan.

Three American operatives. And a Salvadoran national.

Quesada laughed. Before, he fought in their country. Now, they came to him.

They had stepped into the mouth of the devil.

Here, they would die hideously.

12

"What?"

"What did he say?" the newsmen asked one another.

The van driver slammed his door shut. Water streamed from his yellow plastic hat. In the minute that he had stood outside with the Salvadoran army officer, the rain had soaked his clothing. Rain hammered on the sheet metal of the passenger van in an unrelenting, overwhelming noise.

Outside, through the sheets of water pouring over the windows, they saw only darkness and smears of light. The headlights of a truck illuminated a blur of rain, thousands of tiny points scratching against the darkness. Where a searchlight shone on the road and the hillsides, they saw smears of mud brown and gray green. At the end of the two-hour drive over washboard roads, they had expected to photograph burned trucks and bodies. But they saw only rain and mud.

The driver shouted over the rain noise. "He say we go back."

"I'm with the *New York Times*! Who does that beaner think he is?"

"Did you tell him the international correspondent of *People* magazine wanted to interview him?"

"How much money does he want?" another reporter shouted out.

"What's he trying to hide?"

"Misters!" The middle-aged, graying driver shouted them down. "He says we go, we go."

"We don't pay you to drive us around in the rain! We want copy and we want photos."

Starting the van's engine, the driver ended the argument. "Mister, I want to live. *El capitán* says go, I go."

A very overweight young reporter with United Press International slammed his fist into the seat. The reporter's jowls went red with anger and frustration. He slammed his fist into the seat again and again. "Another wasted day!"

"We should have gone with José," an older journalist said.

"To visit his girlfriend and her family?" A reporter in the next seat asked with a sneer. "You want to spend a week in some godforsaken village with mud up to your ass?"

A kilometer past the village of Lolotiquillo, the young Puerto Rican they knew as José Lopez had taken his backpack and stepped out. "See you next week. My amiga lives here." Then he had shouldered his pack and followed a narrow trail toward a cluster of plank and sheet-tin shacks.

"Maybe you could get exclusive interviews," the fat UPI reporter suggested, "with the pigs and flies."

Light flashed in the back window as the second van followed them down the road. Ahead, their headlights shone into a tunnel of rain and mud. Despite the rain, the air inside the van remained sultry. The reporters and photographers sweated in their seats.

They had left Gotera an hour before dark. Because the vans lacked the heavy-duty suspension and powerful engines of the army troop trucks, the road had forced the hired drivers to slow to only a few kilometers per hour to bump over the rocks and ruts. But knowing a scene of terror and murder awaited their cameras and notebooks made the ride worthwhile. Now the frustrated newsmen knew they faced another hour or two in the storm, then an uncomfortable night on the floors of an abandoned hotel. All for nothing.

Lurching and rocking, the van followed the muddy track across the hill. A lightning flash startled the group.

"This is too much rain," the driver shouted back to them. "Too late in year. Very bad for roads."

"What about the international flights?" one journalist shouted out. "Think there'll be flights out tomorrow?"

"If the rain stops," the driver answered.

"Flying out?" a photographer asked the journalist.

"Damn right. I don't get paid unless I file. I'll bounce over to Lebanon and get a story. I'm tight with the Christian militia—"

"The Druze too?"

"All of them. Depends on who I'm talking to. I'll file a story on anyone who's killing people. Maybe I'll go to Libya and see what's doing. There's got to be a war somewhere."

"There's one here. Somewhere."

Guiding the van slowly around a curve, the driver suddenly stomped on the brake.

"What's the problem?"

"What's happening?"

Flicking on the interior light, the driver raised his hands and put his palms against the windshield.

A black form stepped through the headlights.

The journalists saw a rain-soaked black-uniformed man with a rifle. The man wore a black bandana over his face to cover his features. Only his eyes showed.

In the van's second seat, an American journalist who had covered NATO maneuvers recognized the black-clad soldier's rifle as a U.S. Army weapon: an M-16 automatic rifle fitted with an M-203 grenade launcher.

And in a custom plastic and spring-steel shoulder holster, the man wore a NATO prototype weapon distinguished from all other autopistols by the extended magazine and fold-down off-hand grip-lever: a Beretta 93-R with a sound suppressor.

The journalist knew he now witnessed an international headline. This black-uniformed soldier did not represent any of the Salvadoran guerrilla factions. But the American journalist did not speak to the others. He had his own career to advance. This might get him a Pulitzer Prize. Maybe a few appearances on morning talk shows.

Slipping the lens cap off his motorized Nikon, he set the focus ring at three feet and the f-stop at 1.8. He flicked the camera's exposure-mode to automatic. He braced the camera on the seat in front of him and waited to photograph the man he knew to be an American commando illegally operating in the mountains of Morazan.

The black-clad American went to the driver's door and motioned for the driver to roll down the glass. While the rain poured through the open window, the American and the driver whispered together.

The journalist touched the camera's button. He heard the shutter click open. He held the camera absolutely still as it took an electronically metered exposure of the soldier's face in the window.

"¡Gracias a Dios!" the driver exclaimed. *"¡Gracias por su ayuda! Mi esposa y mis niños—"*

"De nada," they all heard the commando say. *"No es necesita a morirse ustedes en esta guerra."*

Then the commando left. As he passed through the headlights, the journalist adjusted the focus and snapped two more photos.

"We stop here," the driver announced. He motioned downhill. "If we go, we die. *Terroristas* wait—"

The driver saw the journalist snapping photos of the departing commando.

Rounding the curve, the second van's headlights revealed another black-clad commando with an autoweapon. Both men returned to the night and rain, suddenly gone.

Before the journalist could protect the camera, the driver got up, went to him and snatched the Nikon from his hands. The driver then turned and slammed the camera against the dash, again and again. He tore open the film door. A coil of film came out. The driver tossed the smashed camera out the window.

For a second, the journalist only stared at the driver. Then the American newsman screamed, "You know what you've done? That was a United States Army Special Forces commando! Operating in a war zone! In violation of congressional prohibitions! Those photos would have been on the front page of every newspaper in the world! You are fired! You have just lost your job. You will never work again for the news services. You are out of work!"

The driver smiled. The smile became a chuckle, then a laugh." *Sí, señor.* Perhaps now I have no job. But except for that Yankee soldier—" the driver looked to the darkness where Rosario Blancanales and Carl Lyons had disappeared "—I would have no life."

13

From the tree line behind the abandoned cornfields, Lyons and Blancanales observed the squad of assassins. The steep rise of the forested hillside allowed the Stony men to look down on the fields and farmhouse and road.

Lightning flashes illuminated the scene in stark moments of black and arc-light white. A hundred meters of rotting cornstalks and furrows gone to weeds separated Lyons and Blancanales from the flowing mud of the road. They saw forms with bipod-braced auto-weapons sprawled here and there in the tangles of rotting cornstalks. Quesada's militiamen wore black fatigues and black web-gear. Some wore black vinyl raincoats and hats. One man stood on the rise, watching the mountain road for headlights.

Tire tracks cut across the abandoned fields to the farmhouse. A small bus, out of view of the road, parked against the rear of the burned-out house; the overhang of the roof sheltered the passenger door from the downpour. The driver's window viewed the hills. Inside the bus, a cigarette lighter flared.

Lightning flashes revealed a man in a black raincoat walking through the storm. He went from position to position, crouching for a moment with each rifleman. Finally, he disappeared into the darkness of the farmhouse.

"That's the leader," Lyons whispered to his partner. "Checking his squad."

"Perhaps...." Blancanales answered. "And perhaps the leader sent out a soldier to check the line."

While Blancanales whispered orders to Ricardo, Lyons checked his weapons and gear. He slung his Atchisson over his back and cinched the sling tight. He tightened his bandolier of 12-gauge mags. Checking the MU-50G controlled-effect grenades in his thigh pockets, he felt the casings click together. He reached out to the ferns around him and pulled off fronds. He shoved them in his thigh pockets as padding to eliminate any chance of the grenades betraying him as he moved.

Blancanales went first, Lyons following. The rain pattered on their backs as they snaked through the furrows. They went down the slope, losing sight of the squad and the bus. Cornstalks blocked their line-of-sight. But the cornstalks also screened them from the vision of Quesada's assassins.

Warm mud coated the fronts of their blacksuits. Lubricated with the black slime, they slid through tangles of rotting cornstalks.

Lyons noticed a detail that would have meant nothing to him before his mission to Guatemala only months before: the corn had not been harvested. He felt the rat-gnawed cobs roll under his hands. The campesino who had sown this field and tended the corn for months had lost the harvest to the war. As he continued toward the bullet-pocked and burned-out house, Lyons wondered if the campesino had also lost his life to the war.

Blancanales stopped Lyons with a muddy hand. They lay side by side in the unrelenting downpour, watching the tiny glow of a cigarette scratch the black of a bus window. Inside the bus, the cigarette flared as the smoker took a drag, then the red point inscribed another arc against the black as the smoker let his arm fall.

The Stony men crept forward, slowly easing through the last rows of cornstalks. The bus and farmhouse leaped from the night as lightning flashed above them, Lyons and Blancanales stopping in midmotion. Thunder came an instant later. They eased forward, had to freeze as lightning flashed again.

Only a few steps from the bus, they stopped to watch and listen. They lay in muddy rainwater and tangled cornstalks. Weeds and debris from the burned farmhouse littered the ground separating them from the bus.

The smoker flicked his cigarette butt into the rain. Moments later, he lit another, the lighter's flare like a spotlight on his face. Blancanales and Lyons memorized the man's features: slash lips, a sharp beak of a nose, a square forehead, his hair combed straight back.

Straining their ears, they listened for voices or movement above the incessant drumming of the rain on the sheet metal of the bus. Lyons reached into the mud in front of his face. Though his black bandana covered most of his features, his eyes and a band of skin inches wide remained uncovered. He had darkened his skin with blacking grease, but he took no chances. As he watched the bus and farmhouse for movement, he daubed the fertile black earth of El Salvador on his face. Then he tapped his partner and pointed to the bus.

Blancanales nodded. He slipped out his silenced Beretta as Lyons crossed the three meters to the bus. Lyons kept his belly and face to the mud, sucking in the rich scent of El Salvador with every slow, measured breath. Easing past a twisted sheet of corrugated-steel roofing, Lyons heard boots splash through mud.

Lyons froze. Sounds of splashes and crunching wood reached him. He waited for the voice of alarm or the slaps of Blancanales's subsonic 9mm slugs punching into the death-squad soldier's body.

The boots passed his outstretched arm. Steel tapped sheet metal. He heard voices.

"*¿Vienen?*"

"*No. Jefe, porque no llama el capitán—*"

"*¡Vayase acá. Esperen en su posición!*"

Splashes and kicked trash sounded the militiaman's path around the farmhouse. Lyons waited to the count of sixty before moving again. He silently wormed under the bus. He waited for lightning.

Above him, the metal floor of the bus squeaked as *el jefe* shifted in his seat. Lyons waited, watching the darkness, listening for other movements. On the other side of the bus, a boot scraped. Two men.

The night went white with lightning, two long flashes allowing Lyons to scan the area around the bus. He saw no sentries. Taking his hand-radio off his web belt, he keyed a click code to signal Blancanales.

Thunder blasted away the sounds of the rain and the boots above him. Lyons felt rather than heard the clicks answering his signal. He unwound the earphone wire and plugged the phone into his ear. Then he pulled his modified Colt Government Model from its spring-clip shoulder holster, thumbed back the hammer to full-cock and set the ambidextrous safety-fire-selector.

Blancanales snaked through the mud. A lightning flash exposed him in the open ground. Lyons saw the lines of the M-16/M-203 on his partner's back, but the mud and moldy cornstalks clinging to his blacksuit made Blancanales look like a mound of soil and trash. The instant of light gone, Blancanales lunged across the last two meters, thunder covering the splashing of his hands and feet.

"That's our man up there," Lyons whispered. "I heard that goon call him 'hef-fe.' That means boss, right?"

"You're positive? Couldn't have been a name, like José? Jorge?"

"Most definitely positive. Then the boss ordered him to go back to his position. He said, 'po-ze-shun.'"

"Posición?"

"That's it."

"Then he is our man."

"There's another goon up there with him. We got to wait for one of them to step out. We only want the number-one goon."

"We should confirm that second man," Blancanales suggested.

"On my way. Watch my back."

Lyons crabbed under the bus, his modified and sound-suppressed Colt autopistol cocked and locked in his hand. He went to the right rear wheel. The right side of the bus, only a step from the adobe wall of the ruined farmhouse, remained in darkness even when lightning flashed. Rain poured from the corrugated-steel sheets overhanging the bus, water splashing on the roof of the vehicle then flowing down the windows.

His eyes searching the darkness, Lyons eased from under the bus. A sheet of falling water washed over him as he rose to a crouch. His thumb on the safety of the silenced Colt, he listened to the rain beating on the bus and the corrugated steel. He stood and looked through a bus window.

He saw only darkness. At the front, the cigarette still glowed. Lyons waited. The cigarette flared, then dropped as the smoker's hand moved. Lyons waited for lightning.

Metal rasped on metal. Even as Lyons dropped into the mud, his body flowing under the bus, Blancanales hissed a warning. Lyons inched sideways, the Colt pointed outward.

"In the field," Blancanales whispered.

Lyons switched the Colt from his right to his left hand. He watched as a shadowy form shifted within the darkness. Lightning flashed.

In the instant of brilliance, they saw Ricardo on his hands and knees in the mud. His eyes startling white against his grease-blackened face, he looked around for death-squad sentries. As the thunder rolled, he scurried up to Lyons and Blancanales through the mud and trash to concealment under the bus.

Whispered Spanish invective greeted him. Lyons listened as Blancanales quietly vented his anger at the teenager's disobedience. He had been instructed to stay in place at the tree line. But Ricardo interrupted the North American commando.

Lyons listened as the two whispered back and forth in Spanish.

Thumping on the soaked earth, many booted feet ran to the bus. The amber light of a battery lantern shone on the mud. Shouts came. A voice in the bus answered. Lyons heard the boots of the militiamen splashing around the bus. Blancanales and Ricardo eased over to Lyons. As the death squad crowded around the bus, Blancanales briefed him in an almost inaudible whisper.

"The army's here. Ricardo saw the trucks coming, so he came to warn us. That's the captain and a sergeant and two or three of the Quesada men out there. They don't understand where the two vans of journalists could have gone."

"What are they doing now?"

"*El jefe* said he would radio for instructions. We'll have to wait."

"Damn right. Can't go anywhere."

Flashes of white light revealed muddy boots around the bus. Yellow light from the battery lantern glistened on the stock of an M-50. Lyons identified the Salvadoran soldiers by their green-patterned camouflage fatigues, the death squad of Quesada militiamen by their black fatigues.

Lyons studied the black fatigues. He realized they were not black, but gray. The gray cloth appeared black because of the soaking rain and the slime.

Gray, Lyons thought, like the uniforms of the army of Unomundo, the would-be Nazi dictator of Guatemala. As here in Morazan, the assassins loyal to Unomundo operated in the gray uniforms of a private army. The mercenary army of criminals and psycho racists hired and equipped by Unomundo even wore the same black nylon boots and web gear as Quesada's gray-uniformed militiamen.

Lyons remembered the capitol reception where right-wing Salvadorans thought to be linked to Unomundo— the Stony Man intelligence sources had found no conclusive proof—laughed with United States senators and congressmen. Young Salvadoran soldiers in expensive suits had served as bodyguards for the wealthy Salvadorans at the high-society party. Later that same week, Able Team encountered those young Salvadoran soldiers in California. Mack Bolan had assigned Able Team to protect the Riveras, a family of Salvadoran refugees who had witnessed the murder of a North American journalist in Sonsonate province. Able Team fought death squads dispatched by Roberto Quesada to pursue and execute the Riveras before they could testify. Looking down at the face of a dead Salvadoran soldier sprawled in a Los Angeles street, Lyons had guessed the connection. An investigation spanning months and the uniforms surrounding him now confirmed his suspicions.

Quesada served Unomundo.

But that knowledge meant nothing if he died tonight. Lyons hissed to Blancanales, "What goes?"

"Quiet. . . ."

Only two steps away, *el jefe* and *el capitán* talked. Blancanales and Ricardo listened. *El jefe* shouted an order to his squad. Around the bus, the boots scrambled. The Salvadoran army soldiers left. Soldiers shouted out their leader's order to the assassins scattered in the roadside fields. At the road, the engines of the troop carriers roared.

Blancanales gave Lyons a hurried briefing. "Quesada canceled the ambush. He has ordered all the men back to the *finca*. Immediately."

Boots banged up the two steps of the passenger entry. Other boots rasped on the cargo ladder at the back of the bus. Men stowed gear on the rooftop rack.

The starter solenoid snapped into the gears to turn over the engine. The engine revved.

"Señors! Nos estamos. . . . " Ricardo started to panic, his words coming in a rush. If the militiamen crowding into the bus had not been talking and banging equipment, they would have heard the frightened boy below them.

"He thinks we're trapped," Blancanales said into Lyons's ear. "And we are. What if we just stay where we are, let them drive away. And pray to God they don't back out."

"No way. We're going with them. To Quesada."

14

Its engine raced as the levers and springs of the vehicle's clutch operated only inches above their faces. The headlights and amber running lights flicked on. Diesel exhaust swirled around Lyons and Blancanales and Ricardo where they lay trapped under the bus.

Lyons threw himself onto his back, the muzzle of his slung Atchisson digging into the mud. The hot exhaust pipe touched his soaked sleeve with a hiss of steam. He glanced at the double rear wheels, judging their path.

Ricardo attempted to crawl clear. Blancanales jerked him back, shoved him sideways to lie next to Lyons. Lyons grabbed Ricardo's muddy shirt to hold him still. Blancanales gave the teenager quick instructions in Spanish as he positioned himself.

The wheels had settled into the mud. Gunning the engine, the driver rocked the bus forward. The gears clanked as the driver shifted into reverse. As the bus rolled back, the engine roared to make torque.

Put it in forward, go straight ahead, Lyons screamed silently. *I don't want to die tonight, because I don't want to leave Unomundo alive.*

The gears clashed again and the bus lurched forward. The wheels rolled through the ruts, splashing water and mud. Lyons and Blancanales prepared to grab the rear bumper. Ricardo stared around him, panicked, his left hand in the mud, his right shielding his face from the hot exhaust blasting into his face. Lyons elbowed Ricardo, jerked his left arm up. He held the boy's wrist as the undercarriage moved over them. Lyons felt a tire brush his shoulder.

Rain struck their faces as the rear bumper cleared them. Lyons slapped Ricardo's hand onto the slick steel of the bumper, then clawed for his own handhold. His fingers hooked around the sharp inside edge. The bus pulled him to a sitting position and he stood.

In the red glow of the taillights, Lyons saw that the bus had two roof access ladders, one on each side of the rear emergency door. He grabbed a ladder and stepped onto the bumper. He stayed low, below the level of the rear windows. The clouding diesel smoke swirled red in the rain.

Blancanales moved as quickly, grabbing first the bumper, then climbing hand over hand up the first three rungs of the ladder.

But Ricardo desperately held the bumper. He let the bus drag him. Lyons hooked an arm through the rungs of the roof ladder and reached down to grab Ricardo's left wrist again. As soon as Blancanales had secured his own handhold, he took Ricardo's other arm. The two men jerked the youth up and steadied him until he braced his sneakers on the bumper.

Whining in first gear, the bus rocked over the cornfield. The three uninvited passengers clung to the rain-slick ladders.

Hundreds of meters down the road, the taillights of the troop trucks disappeared around a mountainside.

Lyons looked over to Blancanales and pointed up. Blancanales shook his head no. The Puerto Rican held up a hand and made the Mexican gesture of "wait a moment," his thumb and forefinger an inch apart. Lyons nodded.

The bus turned onto the road, dropping down a slight

embankment with a final violent swaying on its springs. They heard equipment on the bus roof crash from one side to the other. Straightening the wheels, the driver shifted and accelerated over the flooded road, the bus throwing waves of muddy rainwater into the fields.

Blancanales made a thumbs-up gesture. Lyons pointed to himself, then pointed out. He wiped his palms clean of mud as best he could before easing his head up to the window.

Inside the bus, soaked militiamen sprawled in the seats. Several cigarettes created a gray pall. Lyons saw the beak-nosed *jefe* and another man standing at the front, examining a map by the light of an electric lantern. They talked with one another and the driver.

Mist formed on the window. Lyons noticed a drop of condensation coursing down the inside of the glass. The sweating men, in their soaked uniforms and boots, had heated the interior with their bodies. The superhumid air condensed on the rain-cooled windows.

Lyons eased down. He signaled Blancanales with the Mexican "wait a moment" hand gesture. Blancanales nodded. For another minute or two, they squatted on the bumper, swaying as the bus low-geared through mud and flowing streams. Ricardo crouched, stricken with fear, close to the ladder that held Blancanales.

In the light from the bus headlights, Lyons watched the roadsides. They passed burned-out shacks and the ruins of small farms. Unharvested corn and vegetables rotted in the fields. A cluster of small whitewashed crosses had been placed in front of a charred house.

A dead family, Lyons thought. Maybe they made the mistake of talking democracy, maybe they talked socialism. Maybe they didn't talk at all. Maybe they only wanted to live and work their fields without ideology. So they died.

As the pathetic vignette of tragedy returned to the night, Lyons eased his head up again. He saw the window had fogged over. He signaled Blancanales. Lyons checked his nightsuit and bandoliers for any loose gear that might strike the ladder's steel rungs. Then he went up, his neoprene-soled boots squeaking faintly on the slick steel.

He crawled onto the roof, forcing himself to move slowly, to distribute his weight on the sheet metal without the roof buckling or popping. He turned slowly and looked down to Blancanales and Ricardo. Blancanales whispered a last instruction to the teenager, then prodded him up.

Ricardo moved quickly and silently, his teeth clenched now with determined courage. He scrambled onto the roof. Lyons motioned him flat. The teenager obeyed instantly. As the bus swayed, he sideslipped down the rain-slick enamel of the roof. He reached out with a hand and a foot and braced himself against the cargo rack's side rail.

A moment later, Blancanales followed.

"No problems?" Lyons whispered.

"I had my ear against the bus. No noise, no questions."

"All right! We're on our way." Lyons crept across the roof to bundles of gear. He checked the bundles by touch. He felt plastic and cloth in one. Tents? Camouflage tarps for the bus? His hands found heavy boxes— perhaps boxes of ammunition. Leaning against the bundles, he hooked his boots around the cargo rail.

Loosing the sling, he eased his Atchisson off his back. He checked the safety, then dropped out the magazine and pocketed it. He pulled back the actuator to eject the chambered shell into his hand. The action locked back. He put a finger in the chamber and felt gritty mud.

He turned the autoshotgun muzzledown and shook it. A plug of mud plopped out of the barrel. Hinging the weapon open, he held the receiver group to the sky, letting the rain wash the mechanism. Then he turned the chamber upward. With his cupped hand, he funneled rainwater into the chamber. Rain poured into the barrel and flowed out the muzzle.

In instants of lightning white, Blancanales watched, smiling. "Not the way to clean a weapon, mister."

"Then pass me your cleaning rod."

"Didn't bring one."

"I suggest you check your own barrel for obstructions."

"Next time you go for a roll in the mud," Blancanales instructed his partner in a whisper, "use a rubber band to secure a bit of cellophane or plastic over the barrel. Trick I learned in the monsoons."

"You got cellophane over the barrel of your two-oh-three?"

"No."

In a flash of lightning, he saw Blancanales cleaning mud out of his M-203 grenade launcher.

With a low laugh, Lyons snapped the Atchisson closed. He slipped the shell into the chamber and eased the bolt closed. Slapping in the magazine, he slung the autoshotgun over his shoulder and checked the auto-Colt and Colt Python. He continued his preparation by touch-checking his bandolier of ammunition and the grenades in his pockets.

When they went through the gates of the plantation-fortress, he would need all his firepower. No doubt about it.

Beside him, he heard Blancanales whispering into his hand-radio, "Wizard. Wizard. Political here."

Lyons monitored the transmission on his own radio.

He heard Blancanales's voice. But only snatches of static answered. Blancanales tried key code.

Static-distorted clicks answered. Blancanales keyed out a series of clicks. A series of clicks answered.

"The mountain and the electrical storm are breaking up the signal," Blancanales explained. "But he knows we're okay."

"What happens when we go in?" Lyons asked.

"You suggested this. Don't you have a plan?"

"Haven't had the time to think that far ahead."

Blancanales laughed softly. "Then give it some thought. You're running out of time."

"The radio down there. This is the gang the Wizard monitored, right?"

"Most likely."

"So I figure their radio's the same as the black box we found in the jeep. We'll send out a call to Gadgets and the lieutenant. They'll monitor it on the jeep's radio."

"But if it's like the one we captured, it has a coded digital lock."

"Oh, yeah.... Ah, I don't know what—"

"Face it, Carl. We'll be on our own. Consider that before you open fire."

"Yeah, yeah. But this ride is our ticket into the plantation. We got the chance to grab Quesada and drag him out."

"Remember what the lieutenant told us. Concentric rings of defenses, electronic security, mines, bodyguards and militia on the inside, army react-units on call. Against two of us."

"All those defenses face out," Lyons said pointedly. "We're going in quiet. If we can take Quesada, they won't know what's happening until it's too late."

"We...shall...see...." Blancanales pronounced.

Taillights flashed ahead. Simultaneously, Lyons and

Blancanales went flat, pressing themselves against the bundles of cargo. Brakes squealed.

The bus sounded its airhorn. Soldiers shouted back. Downshifting with a lurch, the bus slowed to a crawl. Lyons looked over the side.

A rush of black water surged against the side of the bus. Branches and forest flotsam struck the sheet metal. The engine revved and the bus tilted upward. The taillights lit a wash of rocks and broken concrete.

With a roar of engines, the troop trucks ahead picked up speed. The clouds of diesel soot stank even in the continuing downpour. The bus driver floored the accelerator and slammed through the gears.

Bouncing and shuddering on the flooded road, the bus raced the trucks. Lights appeared to one side. Lyons saw a lantern on the steps of a turquoise cantina. Headlights revealed whitewashed buildings and a narrow street paved with stones.

The bus swerved and accelerated. Lyons pressed himself to the roof and watched with one eye as the bus paralleled the troop trucks.

Quesada's assassins shouted from the bus windows, laughing and jeering at the soldiers. In the backs of the open trucks, with only plastic tarps around their shoulders to shelter them from the storm, the soldiers returned the jeers. Like two competing sports teams, the militiamen and the soldiers cursed one another and urged their drivers faster. The bus passed one truck, then the other.

Headlights illuminated the back of the bus. Belching diesel smoke, the bus pulled ahead of the trucks. The bus shook and rattled as it hurtled downhill. The tires sprayed mud higher than the windows. Careering through curves, the bus left the trucks far behind.

But other taillights appeared. Lyons raised himself to

look ahead. In the headlights of the bus, he saw a jeep with M-60 machine guns mounted on pedestals, one in the front seat aiming forward, the other in the back. Four soldiers rode in the jeep.

The jeep's brake lights flashed. The bus slowed. The jeep whipped through a turn, the bus following a moment later. Now the vehicles traveled on a paved road.

Kilometers away, the lights of a small city shimmered through the rain and wind. Lyons heard rumbling and squeaking. He looked back to see the troop trucks pass the turnoff without slowing. He nudged Blancanales to rise.

"Can't be San Francisco Gotera," Blancanales told him. "The town hasn't had electricity for years."

"Ricardo!" Lyons hissed.

The teenager spoke quickly to Blancanales. Blancanales turned to Lyons.

"That's the plantation," he said. "What happened back there on the road?"

"They had a race. That's a jeep up front there. I think it's the army officers. The troop trucks went straight. Going back to the garrison, I guess."

"Like at the farmhouse." Blancanales considered what he had observed. "The soldiers stay in the trucks, the officers work with the militia leaders. Perhaps the officers will be meeting with Quesada."

On the paved road, the jeep and bus maintained a steady hundred kilometers per hour. Only a few minutes after they left the mountain road, they saw the lights of a guard tower. The jeep slowed. Taking a last look, the two men of Able Team saw a sentry open a chain link gate topped with razor wire.

Praying that the guard in the watchtower could not distinguish their forms among the bundles and boxes of gear, Lyons and Blancanales and the teenage Ricardo pressed themselves flat on the roof of the bus. The vehicle slowed to a crawl as it lurched over a series of speed bumps. Voices called out, then the bus accelerated again, following a hundred meters behind the jeep.

They sped through the defenses of the Quesada family. When distance reduced the lights of the watchtower to a smear in the rain, Lyons moved to the edge of the roof. Below, the rain-polished asphalt blurred past at a hundred kilometers per hour.

"Pol! Ready to jump? First chance we get."

Blancanales spoke quickly with Ricardo. The teenager crawled to the edge and looked down. He looked at the two North Americans. *"Este es loco...."*

"Sí, mucho loco," Blancanales answered. *"Pero no hay otro cosa a hacer."*

Mercury-arc lights on poles lit the road. Chain link and barbed-wire fences flashed past. Beyond the fences, a few lights shone from the shanties of lumber and tar paper that housed the plantation's field workers. Aluminum prefabs sheltered the overseers guarding the campesinos. But none of the miltiamen in the guard posts braved the storm.

On the other side of the road, rows of coffee bushes extended to the distance. Lyons pointed to the coffee fields.

"In there."

"If you jump now," Blancanales warned him, "with those lights, at this speed, you're dead twice."

"They've got to slow down sometime. First time there's enough darkness to cover us...."

The jeep and the bus continued at a hundred kilometers per hour on the brightly lit service road. Ahead, they saw a cluster of prefab buildings. Lights blazed over an asphalted area crowded with parked trucks and farm equipment.

Lyons cursed. "Slow down! Give us some shadows!" he hissed.

As if the driver had heard, the bus slowed. Lyons braced himself to jump. Blancanales pulled him back, and down.

"Guards, there!"

Two militiamen in yellow raincoats opened the chain link and razor-wire gates to the vehicle yard. The jeep went through the gate. The bus slowed, but too late. It entered the vehicle yard.

The three intruders on the cargo rack went flat. Around them, they saw garages and parked trucks. Sentries paced the asphalt. The hammering of an air ratchet stopped as mechanics watched the returning squad from open-sided service buildings. In the brilliance of thousand-watt lights, nothing in the vehicle yard went unobserved.

As the bus slowed to a stop, men from the death squad stepped out of the passenger door. They called out to the militiamen. The army officers in the jeep drove on to one of the prefabs.

Lyons and Blancanales and Ricardo waited. The militiamen had stowed equipment on the bus roof. The militiamen would unload the equipment.

Flat on their bellies, Lyons and Blancanales unslung their assault weapons. They waited for the sound of boots on the steel rungs of the ladders.

15

Another rattle of static came from the hand-radio. Gadgets Schwarz listened for code-clicks or the voices of his partners. But the electronic noise obscured any message. Gadgets keyed a response. The bursts of static continued.

As rain beat on the plastic tarp sheltering him, Gadgets strained his ears to decipher a message within the static. He fought panic as his imagination created a thousand horrors his partners could have suffered in the hours since they left.

On the captured black radio, he and Lieutenant Lizco had monitored Quesada's cancellation of the ambush and the order for the squad to return to the *finca*.

Then Quesada warned his squad of assassins of the North American paramilitary agents.

How did Quesada know? Gadgets and Lieutenant Lizco had monitored not only the encoded Quesada communications but also the army frequencies. There had been no transmissions from the army react-force sent to collect the casualties and survivors of the guerrilla ambush. Only those soldiers had seen Able Team. Furthermore, Quesada's warning to his militiamen never mentioned ''North American mercenaries en route to Honduras.''

Had one of Quesada's units captured or killed Gadgets's partners?

Blancanales and Lyons had checked in several times.

When they had reached the crest of the mountain. After they had warned the journalists. And when they spotted the death squad.

No more messages came after that. Only a brief and uncertain exchange of static and clicks. Gadgets had responded to the noise by keying clicks in Morse code. But he received no return message or even a confirmation of his Morse signals.

Now more static-blurred clicks came from his radio, in no code or intelligent sequence.

He did not want to believe what his imagination told him about the transmissions: Blancanales or Lyons lay bleeding in some tangle of brush, too badly wounded to put out a coherent message....

Or someone played with the radios. The death squad had captured, maybe killed his partners and now the Salvadoran fascists experimented with the high-tech equipment.

Logically, he knew of many reasons for the breakdown in communication. Distance. The electrical interference of the storm. Damage to the radios.

The distance and lightning had not disrupted the check-in transmissions. Blancanales's voice had come through clear. And too much time had passed since Quesada recalled his death squad. With the help of Ricardo to guide them, Gadgets and Lyons should have reached the top of the mountain, with or without a prisoner. Only the possibility of damage remained. But both radios damaged? Or one destroyed and the other damaged? Unlikely.

He had to know.

In the makeshift tent made by throwing a plastic tarp over the jeep and the pedestal-mounted M-60, he put his feet up on the jeep's dashboard and considered the problem. He had few options. He and the lieutenant could not leave this position to search for his partners.

That left him with an electronic option. Boost the signal strength of his hand-radio. Could he use the long-distance transmitter with which they would signal Jack Grimaldi, the ace Stony Man pilot, in Honduras? No. That radio only transmitted digital code pulses on an ultra-high frequency. But Gadgets had other radios available. Pushing aside the tarp, he called into the rain and darkness.

"Lieutenant!"

The Salvadoran appeared. He had stood guard in the rain since nightfall. "Another radio message?"

"*Nada.* And man, that suggests a mucho bad problem."

Gadgets hooked a penlight to the dash. In the weak light, he searched through his kit and pulled out rolled metallic tape antenna. The antenna went with the ultra-high-frequency, long-distance transmitter. He kept one end and gave the lieutenant the roll. "This is an antenna. It has to go up the mountain."

Lieutenant Lizco nodded and disappeared into the downpour.

Opening the army radio console, Gadgets spliced the tape antenna's wires into the radio's antenna leads. Then he opened the case of his hand-radio. In the next few minutes, working carefully and exactly in the dim light, he wired the hand-radio's output with the microphone inputs of the army radio.

The army radio now served as a signal booster for the small hand-radio. The radio's encoded milliwatt output would be amplified by the high-wattage circuits of the army transmitter. With the jeep's whip antenna and the hundred feet of wire serving as a second antenna, Gadgets had a chance of overcoming distance and the storm's electrical interference to reach his partners' radios.

Looking into the darkness again, he called out, "Lieutenant! You got that antenna up there?"

Cold metal touched his ear. He knew what touched him even as he turned, infinitely slowly, to look.

The muzzle of an autorifle.

16

With the silenced Colt Government Model cocked and off safety in his hand, Lyons waited. Blancanales held his Beretta 93-R in one hand, his radio in the other. He desperately clicked the transmit key again and again, whispering into the microphone on the wild hope that he could raise Gadgets.

Blancanales and Lyons and Ricardo needed help. They needed a diversion. Anything.

They lay flat on the roof of the bus, waiting. Below them, the militiamen left the bus. They talked and joked with the sentries.

The bus had stopped in the center of the vehicle yard. Thirty meters of naked pavement surrounded the bus on all sides. A blacktop killing ground.

Lyons hoped to silently kill the men who came up to unlash the gear on top of the bus. But any noise or shout of alarm would trigger the firefight. And with the first burst of shots, Able Team lost any possible chance to kidnap Colonel Quesada.

Let alone live.

Waiting for the sound of boots on the steel rungs of the ladders, Lyons eased the MU-50G controlled-effect grenades out of his thigh pocket with his left hand. The tiny grenades, designed for the close-quarter combat of anti-terrorist actions, had a forty-six gram charge of TNT to propell 1400 steel balls. The reduced charge of explosive limited the hundred percent kill diameter to ten meters.

He passed the grenades to Ricardo. They had not allowed their teenage prisoner to carry a rifle. Lyons wished they had issued him one of the M-60s from the jeeps, with a thousand rounds of 7.62mm NATO. When the action started, it would be the Atchisson and the M-16/M-203 against every weapon of the Quesada militia.

They felt the bus shudder. Spewing diesel soot, the engine started again. The driver put the bus in gear and eased it toward a line of trucks. The squad of militiamen walked toward the prefab buildings.

"We got a chance," Lyons whispered to his partner. "We got a chance."

"Perhaps. . ." Blancanales answered.

The driver maneuvered the bus into a space between another bus and a truck. As the brakes squeaked with the stop, the intruders on the cargo rack felt the bus rock.

Now, boots came up the ladder.

As the militiaman's yellow rain hat appeared, Lyons lunged out and grabbed the man's raincoat. He jerked the militiaman's face against the suppressor of the auto-Colt and pulled the trigger.

The 185-grain slug smashed through the militiaman's eye socket at 1000 feet per second, liberating 400 foot-pounds of shockforce within the cranium. Blood and gray matter sprayed Lyons, bits of brain and bone and hair exploding into the rain. Lyons and Blancanales pulled the corpse onto the cargo rack.

"His raincoat, the hat, his uniform," Lyons hissed. "All of it. Get it on the kid."

Blancanales nodded. After explaining to Ricardo in Spanish, they stripped the corpse. Blood from the shattered skull colored their hands. Rain washed away the blood.

Ricardo took the dead man's web-gear and bandolier of autorifle magazines. Then the gray fatigue shirt. Then the boots and pants.

"Mario!" a voice called from below.

"Get the kid into that uniform!" Lyons whispered urgently.

The boots did not fit. Ricardo pulled on the gray pants. In the gray uniform and black web-gear, Ricardo looked like a Quesada militiaman.

Slipping out his Beretta 93-R, Blancanales returned to Lyons at the cargo rail. He pointed to his Beretta. Lyons nodded and put away the auto-Colt. They waited. The voice called out again.

"Mario!"

Another pair of boots came up the ladder. Lyons waited until the militiaman started over the rail, then clutched him simultaneously at the collar and the belt. The death squadder knew only an instant's panic before Blancanales put the Beretta to the side of the man's head and punched a 9mm hole through his temple.

The militiaman, one of the assassins from the mountain ambush, wore a black raincoat and hat over his gray uniform. His boots fit Ricardo. Blancanales put on the black slicker and hat to cover his nightsuit and weapons.

"You take the yellow raincoat and hat," Blancanales told Lyons.

A minute later, they climbed down the ladders to the blacktop. Across the service yard, the sentries stood with the mechanics in the shelter of the open-sided garage buildings.

An M-16 leaned against the bumper. Blancanales reached to the militia web-gear Ricardo now wore. The bandolier held M-16 magazines. He passed the rifle to the teenager.

With the hesitance and great care of someone recently trained, Ricardo double-checked the safety and the seating of the magazine, then eased back the bolt to peek at the round in the chamber. Lyons and Blancanales nodded their approval of this novice's good sense.

Lyons walked along the side of the bus, the yellow raincoat covering his slung Atchisson and gear. He also held the silenced auto-Colt under the raincoat. Glancing through the windows, he saw *el jefe* working by a battery lantern's light.

Coiling a microphone cord, the death-squad leader returned the "black box" radio to its aluminum-and-foam carrying case. Lyons saw no one else in the bus. Looking back, Lyons motioned to Blancanales.

"What?" Blancanales asked, joining him beside the passenger door of the bus.

"The number-one goon," Lyons whispered. "With the NSA radio."

Blancanales snatched a look through the window. "How convenient. We take him."

"And he takes us to Quesada," Lyons added.

Metal squeaked. Footsteps crossed the bus. Lyons and Blancanales pressed themselves against the side. Blancanales pointed to Lyons, closed his hand into a fist. He touched his chest, then pointed to the Beretta he held. Lyons nodded and holstered his auto-Colt.

Carrying the aluminum case, *el jefe* stepped from the bus. Blancanales jammed the Parkerized black suppressor of the Beretta under his chin. As the death-squad leader jerked back reflexively, Lyons pinned the man's arms.

"Silencio," Blancanales warned. He took the radio case out of their prisoner's hand. Lyons jerked his arms behind him and secured his wrists with plastic handcuffs.

Ricardo whistled. Headlights flashed through the falling rain. They saw the Salvadoran army jeep speeding to the bus.

Blancanales spoke in quick Spanish to *el jefe*.

The death-squad leader clamped his jaw and said nothing. Blancanales emphasized his question by putting the Beretta to the man's beak nose. *El jefe* spoke in German-accented English.

"What do you want?"

"Quesada."

El jefe's lips drew back in a sardonic grin. "How interesting."

"You want to live?" Lyons demanded. "You're taking us to Quesada."

"Certainly."

Glancing to the approaching headlights, Blancanales told the prisoner, "You move, you try to warn them, you die."

He left Lyons with the prisoner. Putting his auto-Colt to the back of *el jefe*'s head, Lyons grunted, "Where you from?"

"From Salvador, *americano*."

"Why do you have an accent?"

"I learned English at a German university. Why do you ask?"

As the jeep stopped behind the bus, the army officer called out to Blancanales in Spanish. Blancanales answered as he stepped toward the officer. The officer questioned Blancanales. Even as the officer spoke, he went for the holstered pistol under his raincoat.

Blancanales brought up the Beretta. Firing silent three-shot bursts, the slugs slapping into their chests and faces with a sound like quick fists, he killed the officer and two soldiers in the jeep before their hands closed on their weapons. He moved to the driver's seat.

Pushing the dead soldier aside, Blancanales got in and backed the jeep through a quarter turn. The headlights now pointed toward the prefabs two hundred meters away, the glare blocking the vision of the mechanics and sentries.

He motioned Ricardo forward. While Lyons held the prisoner, Blancanales and Ricardo jerked the corpses out of the jeep. They carried the bodies a few steps and shoved them under a truck.

Lyons shoved *el jefe* forward. Blancanales sent Ricardo back for the "black box" radio. Then they took seats in the jeep, Blancanales driving, their prisoner in the front passenger seat. Lyons sat directly behind *el jefe*, the auto-Colt against the German-educated Salvadoran's back. Next to the second pedestal-mounted M-60, Ricardo now wore one of the Salvadoran army-issue camouflage green plastic ponchos.

Throwing the jeep into gear, Blancanales accelerated for the gate. He flashed the high beams. As before, the sentries opened the gates. Lyons leaned forward to the prisoner.

"Look straight ahead. Don't even think of making a noise. If you want to live, you're taking us to Quesada."

"I understand," their prisoner answered.

"Which way to Quesada?" Blancanales demanded.

The prisoner nodded to the right. Blancanales sped through the gate, sideskidding on the wet pavement as he made the right turn.

Lyons saw that the service road continued straight for hundreds of meters. Far ahead, taillights blinked and disappeared. No other vehicles traveled the road.

Standing, Lyons checked the jeep's rear M-60. The machine gun had no belt in place. Opening the side-mounted box of ammunition, he found the belts of cartridges dry. He threw open the M-60's feed cover.

In the blue white light from the mercury-arc street-lights over the road, Lyons saw rust in the mechanism. He had no time to clean and oil the weapon. He put a belt in place, shut the feed cover and jerked back the operating handle. A cartridge chambered. He jerked back the operating handle one more time. The cartridge ejected. Maybe the M-60 would fire.

Squinting into the wind-driven rain, he looked at the forward M-60. The second machine gun had no belt of cartridges loaded.

The Salvadoran army officers had entered the free-fire zone without arming their heavy weapons. Not wanting to risk leaning over the fascist prisoner to arm the second machine gun, Lyons sat down. He shouted over the noise of the tires and rain to Blancanales.

"Ask Ricardo what goes on in those mountains. To-day, the Commies hit those troop trucks. The officers in this jeep were part of the react-force. But you know, they went into those mountains unloaded. Neither one of these M-60s had a belt in place."

"What?" Blancanales asked, incredulous.

"Take a look," Lyons said, pointing at the second M-60. "I just loaded the back gun. But that one, it's empty. And I bet you those ammo belts in the can got no rain on them. What do you think of that?"

"Later! Look...."

They approached a landscaped area. Immaculate lawns surrounded a ten-foot-high concrete wall. The modernistic, flowing lines of the cast concrete offered no hand-or toeholds. The lawns, lit bright as day by many lights, provided open fields of fire for the machine guns placed in guard positions built into the wall. No flower beds or decorative greenery offered cover for infiltrators.

A sheet-steel gate barred the entry. A concrete-and-steel security office in the center of a traffic circle blocked the possibility of ramming through the gate. Without artillery or antibunker rockets, the two men of Able Team saw no way in but the steel gate.

Lyons leaned forward to their prisoner. "What's inside?"

"Colonel Quesada," *el jefe* answered. "That is the family compound. Inside, there are homes and offices and the Quesada personal guards. Sóon, you will see."

A Dodge four-door had stopped at the bunkerlike security office. Under glaring lights, the passengers stood in the shelter of an alcove while guards with M-16 rifles searched the car.

One of the passengers wore the uniform of the army of El Salvador.

The other passenger wore fatigues, polished black jump boots and black web-gear. He wore a holstered pistol. A red hammer and sickle marked his shoulder.

"La Víbora!" Ricardo gasped. He pointed at the man in fatigues next to the army officer. "*¡Allá! El es mi capitán, el capitán de la PFL. La Víbora! No es un revolucionario. El es una facista!*"

Slowing to stop behind the Dodge, Blancanales translated for Lyons. "He says that's his officer. The one that got away from us this afternoon."

"The army and the Communists," Lyons said loudly, "going in to visit the colonel. A miracle of Salvadoran politics."

El jefe dived out of the jeep. He smashed into the pavement and rolled.

As Blancanales floored the accelerator and whipped the steering wheel to the left, Lyons saw the guards at the gate startle. The soldiers searching the car turned. Then the broken and bleeding *el jefe* screamed, "*¡Americanos. Matéselos!*"

Autoweapons roared.

17

A line of tracers shot from a slit in the wall. Blancanales careened across the lawn, throwing muddy bluegrass behind the jeep's tires. Lyons fought G-force, one arm around the M-60's pedestal, his free hand grabbing for the pistol-grip of his Atchisson rifle.

But Ricardo was the first to strike back. He jerked the pin from one of the Italian MU-50Gs and threw it at his former guerrilla leader. Before the tiny frag hit, Ricardo pulled the pin on the second. He saw the army officer and La Víbora dropping flat beside the Dodge. He let the lever flip free as he braced for the throw. He turned in his seat and awkwardly, threw the second grenade.

The first grenade bounced off the security-office wall. A guard braced his M-16 on the roof of the Dodge and sighted on the jeep. Popping behind him, the grenade shattered the Dodge side windows and peppered the guard with hundreds of pinpoint wounds. Arching backward in shock, the guard fell, his M-16 spraying wild autofire straight up.

La Víbora dashed for the M-16. The second grenade skipped across the asphalt, then rolled under the Dodge. The army officer saw the tiny grenade and scrambled away on his hands and knees. La Víbora looked down at his feet and saw it.

Hundreds of tiny steel balls slashed his body like razors. Steel punched into his downturned face. The blast knocked his feet from under him. Blinded, his feet ripped to blood-spurting tangles of leather and flesh, he crawled for safety. Dying on the asphalt, his body released an immense blood pool that spread around him.

As Blancanales steered the jeep through a half circle, Lyons untangled his Atchisson from his yellow raincoat. He flipped the fire-selector down to full-auto. Patterns of high-velocity steel swept the guards and the army officer, silencing their weapons.

But the machine gun still fired from the slit in the compound's concrete wall. Lyons knew he had no hope of killing that gunner. From the top of the wall, other weapons flashed. His voice almost lost in the hammering of the machine guns and autorifles, Lyons screamed to Blancanales, "Make distance! Get us out of here!"

Ricardo saw a sentry running along the top of the wall. The young man pointed his M-16. In his panic, he sprayed the entire magazine in one burst. He missed the guard and the wall, and the last three slugs, red tracers, streaked high into the rain.

Slapping another magazine into his Atchisson, Lyons hit the bolt release to strip the first shell into the chamber, then set the safety. He tore off the bright yellow raincoat and let it flutter away. He slipped the Atchisson's sling over his neck so that the autoshotgun hung ready at his right side, then stood up behind the pedestal of the M-60.

The guard on the wall fired down at the jeep. Windshield glass shattered. Lyons sighted on a gray-uniformed militiaman and fired, the burst lifting the man off his feet, tracers passing through his body.

Blancanales skidded through a high-speed turn, and they left the Quesada family compound behind. Now on the plantation service road, Blancanales floored the accelerator. Lyons turned, saw headlights on the road.

"Ricardo!" Lyons shouted. He slapped the M-60.

The teenager understood and moved instantly. Slinging the M-16 as Lyons had slung his autoweapon, the boy stood and took the machine gun's pistol-grip.

Lyons stepped over the seat to the forward gun. He popped open the can of belted ammo, then threw open the machine gun's feed cover. He slapped down the belt of 7.62mm NATO cartridges, jerked back the operating lever and fired.

Under the blue white luminescence of the plantation's lights, the brass casings and belt links shot out in a cascade of glittering metal. Lyons held the sights on the headlights. The line of orange red tracers extended from the jeep to the approaching vehicle. One of the headlights went black. Ricocheting tracers sparked in all directions. Glass sprayed.

The driver died. His Chevy Silverado drifted off the lane of blacktop. Lyons sighted on the doors and put bursts through the body panels. The Silverado crashed into the chain link security fence. Lyons turned as the jeep raced past.

Ricardo fired a long burst into the Silverado. Gasoline flashed, and a fireball churned up into the black sky. No one escaped the burning hulk.

"On the right! *A la derecha!*" Blancanales shouted.

Only a hundred meters ahead, Lyons saw a gray-painted jeep emerging from the darkness of the coffee fields. A militiaman in a black rain slicker swiveled a pedestal-mounted M-60 as Lyons whipped up his Atchisson, thumbing down the fire-selector.

Firing from the hip, Lyons sprayed steel balls at the gunner. The Atchisson's twenty-inch barrel allowed the double-ought and number-two buckshot to disperse in extremely wide patterns. He saw the gunner jolt as one or two balls hit him.

But Blancanales closed the distance at one hundred

fifty kilometers per hour. At ranges of fifty meters and thirty meters, Lyons triggered single shots and hit the gunner again, throwing him backward.

Muzzleblast slammed the back of his head. Reeling with the pain, Lyons sat down hard as Ricardo tore into the militia jeep with slugs from the rear M-60. A line of red tracers passed through the militia jeep's windshield, specks of phosphor spinning into the darkness of the coffee fields.

Ricardo saw Lyons holding his aching ears and realized he had fired the heavy-caliber machine gun only inches above the head of the North American. He leaned to Lyons and gripped his shoulder.

"¡Lo siento, señor! ¿Esta usted okay?"

His ears ringing, Lyons looked back to Ricardo. "No problem! Kill them!"

They left the militia patrol behind. Ricardo swiveled the M-60, walking a circle around the machine gun's pedestal as he fired more bursts into the jeep. The dead driver allowed the jeep to lurch forward to stall in the roadway. Ricardo raised his aim to the headlights following them.

Tracers crisscrossed. In the lead vehicle pursuing them, an experienced gunner got their range. Slugs whined off the roadway beside them. A tracer sparked off a fender. A slug slammed into the jeep's spare tire.

Lyons sighted the Atchisson on the headlights two hundred meters behind them. Then he adjusted his aim upward to compensate for drop. He fired semiauto, once, twice, three times, emptying the Atchisson's box mag.

Behind them, a headlight went black. The lead jeep—with only one headlight—swerved from side to side. The other headlights wove. Though the steel buckshot at that extreme distance presented no lethal threat to their pursuers, the spent projectiles had shattered glass and perhaps wounded the standing machine gunner.

They approached the vehicle yard. Many pairs of headlights indicated a general mobilization of the militiamen.

A truck came from the gate and blocked the road. Letting the Atchisson hang at his side, Lyons put the butt of the forward-pointing M-60 to his shoulder. As Blancanales slowed to evade the roadblock, Lyons sighted carefully and put bursts through the rear tires. The next burst went through the passenger-side door.

Holding the trigger back, Lyons raked the cab, behind the door, under the door, hoping to find the fuel tanks. He scored. The tracers ignited a sea of gasoline. A flaming figure staggered from the inferno and stumbled into the coffee rows to burn. The sheet of flames blocked the vehicle-yard exit.

Lyons directed the line of 7.62mm at the gate, killing a sentry, shattering the windshield of a Silverado blocked by the burning truck. He swept the autofire across the other vehicles attempting to exit—trucks, cars, a bus. Tracers hit the chain link fencing and flew at wild angles. But the fragments and ricocheting heavy NATO slugs retained the velocity to punch through steel and flesh.

Militiamen evacuated their transports. Rifles and heavy weapons returned Lyons's fire as Blancanales left the asphalt road for the muddy coffee fields. Ricardo directed his fire straight back at the vehicle yard, sending a line of tracers through the flames and smoke to rake militiamen and trucks and cars.

Ricochets from wild autofire scratched against the black overcast. The orange glow of the gasoline flames tinted the clouds.

"How we going to get out the gate?" Blancanales shouted to Lyons.

"Only one way. Crash it."

Blancanales downshifted to power through mud and pools of rainwater. "We won't make it. It's steel beams and cables under the chain link."

"You don't think this jeep would do it?"

"If we try to crash that gate with this vehicle," Blancanales emphasized, "we will disable this vehicle. We will be on foot. And then very quickly dead."

"So the solution is obvious. . . ."

Lyons looked back. Headlights followed them along the row of coffee. Ahead, their headlights illuminated a long corridor through endless coffee bushes. Standing in the front seat, he looked over the bushes but saw no roads or breaks in the green sea of the plantation.

Slugs tore past him as the militiamen sighted on their jeep's taillights. Ricardo returned the fire. But with the lurching and bumping of the jeeps and trucks over the earth and mud, no one hit anyone.

Lyons climbed into the back. As Ricardo watched for targets, Lyons pulled his Colt Python. He held the revolver by the barrel and leaned over the tailgate of the jeep. He smashed out the taillights.

Blancanales cut to the left. Crashing across rows, swerving, he zigzagged to confuse the pursuers. He maintained a course parallel to the road, then veered back for the blacktop. Lyons saw headlights in the rows continuing in the opposite direction.

But on the road, headlights waited for them. A truck's spotlight swept the rows of coffee. Lyons motioned Ricardo to the front machine gun. He leaned to Blancanales and explained.

"Here's the plan. Get as close to the road as you can while the kid puts out some rounds. Then turn parallel. Then cut for the road. Got it? Straight on, parallel, then straight on to the road and make it for the gate. I'll be right behind you.''

''What are you talking about?''

''I'm getting us a truck.''

''Crazyman!''

''You got any ideas?'' Lyons touch-checked his equipment. Bandoliers. Pistols. Grenades. Knife.

As they neared the road, the spotlight found them. Autorifles fired. Blancanales switched off the headlights and swerved through bushes. Ricardo aimed the M-60 at the lights. Blancanales spoke to him quickly in Spanish. The teenager raised the barrel and fired a short burst over the truck.

Forms scattered. The searchlight went dark. Lyons tapped Blancanales.

''Now!''

The jeep slowed for a moment. Lyons stepped into the darkness, running for a few steps. He crashed into a bush and rolled through mud. The jeep accelerated away in the darkness, plunging through coffee rows.

Lyons moved fast. Mud sucked at his boots. Ahead, he heard voices. Rifles fired blindly into the coffee rows, the slugs cutting through leaves and branches. He moved closer. He saw militiamen bracing M-16 rifles on the hood of a gray Silverado. They watched the rows for the North Americans.

Lights appeared a hundred meters to his right as Blancanales switched on his headlights. The militiamen at the truck snapped bursts from their M-16s. The jeep's headlights wavered as Blancanales bounced up the shoulder of the service road and skidded through a hard right turn.

Three militiamen scrambled into the Silverado. Lyons, sprinting across the broken, muddy ground, stopped, pulled down a breath to steady his aim and lined up the Atchisson's tritium nightsight on the windows of the truck.

In the front seat, the militiamen died before they heard the shots that killed them. Blasts of steel smashed through the passenger-side window and punched through their skulls. In the back seat, a man's eyes whirled toward the flash in the darkness. Steel balls shattered his window and tore away his head.

Lyons sprinted to the passenger truck, the Atchisson ready in his hands. He fired blasts point-blank into the seats to kill any militiaman waiting to surprise him. But the Silverado contained only corpses. He shoved aside the driver's body and started the truck.

Racing after the jeep, he flicked the high beams again and again. He saw Ricardo aim the M-60 at the Silverado's windshield. Lyons flicked the high beams once more and waved a hand out the window. He accelerated to pass the jeep.

"Stop!" he shouted out to Blancanales.

Blancanales slowed. "What?"

The jeep and the Silverado coasted on the blacktop. Lyons saw the guard tower and gate three hundred meters ahead. He leaned across a gory militiaman to speak to Blancanales through the shattered passenger window.

"You two put out rounds. Get as close as you can risk, and then put out everything you got. Or they're going to chop me to shit before I hit that gate. There are heavy machine guns up there. Maybe rockets."

"Anything you say. This is your idea."

"You first, then I come up to speed."

Blancanales accelerated ahead. Looking in the rearview mirror, Lyons saw headlights weaving through the smoke and the flames far behind him. Other headlights came from the coffee rows.

Tracers arced down from the tower. Blancanales swerved from side to side as Ricardo aimed the M-60's autofire at the gunner. Flame flashed from the tower and a rocket shrieked into the earth. Blancanales slammed to a stop. He snapped up his M-16/M-203 and fired.

A 40mm grenade popped against the tower. The frag did not silence the machine gun. Blancanales aimed the jeep's front M-60. Two streams of tracers found the tower. Lyons saw tracers going in one window and out the other side.

Lyons prepared to crash the gate. He shoved the corpses of the militiamen into the footwell. He kicked one dead man up against the firewall. Then he put the heavy passenger truck into gear and floored the accelerator.

Driving the truck like a missile, he aimed for where padlock and chains secured the gates. A heavy steel crossbar braced them.

The designers of the Quesada security perimeter had anticipated attack from the outside. Therefore they had installed speed bumps in front of the gates to stop vehicles from hurtling into them. But they had not protected the gates from vehicles crashing *out*.

Lyons flashed past the jeep.

The machine gunner in the tower directed his weapon at the racing truck. Tracers sparked off the road.

Two lines of tracers found the machine gunner.

In the Silverado, Lyons held the steering wheel until the last instant, then threw himself against the dead men in the footwell.

The flesh of corpses reduced the shock, but the impact stunned him. At one-hundred-plus kilometers per hour, the Silverado cut its way through the buckling gates, snapped chains, bent the steel crossbar around the truck, threw one gate into the air.

The Silverado survived the crash, but not the speed bumps.

The springs shattered. Wheels smashed into fenders and the axles snapped. When the frame hit the bumps, the Silverado flipped end over end.

Blancanales saw the hulk roll to a stop on its side. He sped to the gate, skidded almost to a stop to negotiate the bumps. Ricardo fired burst after burst, aiming upward through the floor of the tower. No fire answered. Blancanales braked behind the shelter of the mangled truck.

"You alive?" he shouted out.

Lyons struggled to climb out the window. Blancanales grabbed the Atchisson from Lyons's hands, then helped his partner from the wreck. The Ironman stared around him, his eyes unfocused. Gore covered him.

Running his hands over Lyons's arms and legs, Blancanales checked for broken bones. He found only blood and pieces of flesh. Lyons watched him.

"You're wasting time," Lyons said. "That's other people all over me. Check my gear. I got my pistols? Where's my Atchisson?"

"Colt .45. Revolver. Here's the shotgun—"

"Then get me out of here. I am all fucked up," Lyons intoned.

Blancanales half-carried him to the jeep and eased him into the seat. In seconds, they raced away from the *finca*.

Infinitely slowly, Lyons turned in the seat to look back. Flames and columns of black smoke rose from several fires. Gasoline fireballed as he watched.

Two pairs of headlights still pursued them. He slowly turned forward again. He closed his eyes and spoke.

"You know what this means, don't you—"

"Don't talk. You might be broken inside. I'll

give you some morphine when we get back to the Wizard.''

"It means we lost the element of surprise. But I'll get him.''

"What're you talking about? I'm radioing Grimaldi for a medevac.''

Lyons continued as if Blancanales had not spoken. "Now we know what's going on. We know Quesada's in there. But he knows we're out here. Now it's going to be a real drag.''

The M-60 fired, Ricardo hammering the pursuing trucks with slugs. Autorifles sparked and slugs zipped past the jeep. A slug smashed into the tailgate.

Lyons sighed. "More nonsense.''

Rising slowly from the seat, he gripped his Atchisson like a crutch.

"Don't move, don't,'' Blancanales told him. "The boy can handle them. They won't follow us into the mountains. We'll get away, no problem.''

Flashes ripped apart the night. Points of flame from the muzzles of autorifles and squad automatic weapons slashed the darkness. Tracers streaked down at the jeep from the hillside above the road. Hundreds of slugs filled the air.

Ambush.

18

In the communications room, Colonel Quesada keyed the digital code lock to power the high-tech radio. Machine-gun fire continued outside the family compound. The voices of his personal aides called from office to office as his staff marshaled the militia forces. He heard men rushing through the corridor. Colonel Quesada spoke urgently into the microphone of the secure-band American radio.

"Captain Mendez! Captain Mendez! This is Colonel Quesada. Emergency!"

Boots stopped outside the door. A fist knocked. "Colonel! News from the fighting. We have the identities of the attackers."

"Wait. In a moment . . . ."

The colonel knew who attacked. The warning of the North American "paramilitary agents" had come from Washington only hours before. But his friends in the United States administration had said "paramilitary," not "commandos."

The North Americans had endangered his life with the use of the wrong word. In his country, "paramilitary" meant raping and murdering the family of an unarmed campesino, or the driveby machine-gunning of a student at a bus stop, or the torture and mutilation of a teenage girl. Salvadoran "paramilitary agents" did not assault concrete-and-steel defense positions manned by overwhelming numbers of militiamen.

The voice of his trusted officer over the radio interrupted Quesada's panic. "This is Captain Mendez."

"Are your men mobilized?"

"My squad assembles at the helicopters. We will pursue the Communist—"

"No!" commanded Quesada. "Your duty will be my personal security in Honduras. We will go to La Escuela. Tell the pilots to prepare for the flight to Reitoca. We will take two helicopters. Divide your squad into two groups. I will wait in the gardens for my helicopter."

"*Comandante*, the attack is over. The guerrillas have fled the property."

"Then what is that I hear?"

"The militia shoots at shadows and trees. Allow my unit to pursue and exterminate—"

"The attack is not over! They killed my men in San Francisco and Los Angeles, California. And they are not guerrillas. They are elite commandos sworn to my assassination. They will come again."

"These commandos have attacked before? In North America? Now here? *Comandante*, no one informed me of this threat to your security—"

"Ready the helicopters. We leave immediately!"

Colonel Quesada switched off the National Security Agency radio. He pressed an intercom button. "Orderly. Return to your duties."

As the colonel left the communications room, the radio operator ran in from the other office. Colonel Quesada did not allow any of the technicians to remain at the other radios when he used the secure-band radios. The high-tech electronics encoded every transmission to ensure absolute secrecy. But a disloyal radio operator overhearing and repeating a message would negate all the marvels of the North American technology.

A militia officer waited in the corridor, his gray uniform dripping rainwater. He snapped to attention and saluted when he saw his commander. "I have the identities of the attackers, *comandante*."

"Who are they?"

"North Americans. One blue-eyed, the other Latin. The second one speaks Spanish. There is a third, but he is believed to be Salvadoran."

"Did you see them?"

"No. They took Lieutenant Kohl prisoner, but he fought his way free before the attack—"

"Kohl? Him? Take me to him."

The officer nodded. "He is with the wounded. This way, *comandante*...."

Hurrying past the command offices, Colonel Quesada saw his officers speaking into telephones and pointing at maps. Some wore dry uniforms, others muddy fatigues. A radio monitored the walkie-talkie chatter between the scattered militia units. Voices announced a confusion of victories and defeats, casualties and men missing, guerrilla corpses and Communist units trapped in ambushes.

But the noise of machine-gun fire and the panicky voices on the radios had only suggested the truth.

As they stepped from the building, the colonel received his first images of the strike by the North Americans.

To the west, flames tongued the night. Orange light glowed on the storm clouds. Black columns rising from the *finca* merged with the black sky. Despite the continuing rain, the acrid stink of burning fuel and rubber and flesh seared the colonel's throat.

Everywhere on the vast plantation, the hammering of machine guns continued. Tracers arced through the night like penny skyrockets at a saint's festival. He heard the ripping sound of M-16 rifles.

Colonel Quesada followed the officer along the veranda to a garage near the main gate. Holding the door open, the officer announced the colonel's entry.

"Attention! Our commander!"

Stepping into the dim interior, a smell struck Colonel Quesada, a horrible commingled stench of vomit and blood, scorched hair and burned flesh. Medics turned from a gore-red table and saluted with bloody hands. His eyes scanned the carnage on the floor.

Dead and wounded militiamen sprawled everywhere. A line of dead had been piled against one wall. Wounded men writhed on the garage floor, pouring their blood onto the oily concrete. One man had been totally blackened by fire. His eyes and features and fingers gone, he gasped down breaths through a seared throat, yellow fluid bubbling from the ruin of his face when he exhaled.

"How many men dead?" the colonel asked a medic.

"Eight dead, two dying, five wounded."

"Thank God it was not worse," Colonel Quesada told the officer leading him.

The medic corrected his commander. "But these are only the casualties from the compound and the guard posts. They are taking the other wounded to the hospital. And the fighting continues everywhere."

"There is Lieutenant Kohl," the officer pointed.

Stepping over wounded and dying men, they went to a militia officer wrapped in bandages. Splints immobilized his right shoulder and right arm. Blood seeped through the bandages wrapping his head.

Colonel Quesada went to one knee beside Lieutenant Kohl. "Nephew, what happened?"

Kohl, the death-squad leader whom Lyons and Blancanales had called *el jefe*, opened eyes glazed from medication. He tried to sit up. A medic held him down.

Finally, the sharp-featured, light-haired young man spoke.

"We returned from the mountains. In the motor yard...as I left the troop bus, they took me. Two were *gringos*. They spoke gringo English and North American Spanish.... There was a Salvadoran traitor...."

The colonel heard rotorthrob approaching.

"When Captain Lopez came in the jeep...to take me to your meeting...they shot him and his men. I knew if they went to the gate to the family compound, the guards would take them. I sounded the alarm and dived from the car...then there was shooting. I know nothing else."

"Only two?"

"Three...I saw three."

The colonel heard the helicopter descending in the garden. He hurried his questioning. "Only two gringos?"

"A dark one and a blond one."

"A Negro?"

"Not Mexican...Puerto Rican...I do not know. They covered their faces. I only guess."

"Comandante!" Captain Mendez called from the door. "There is a development in the battle!"

Colonel Quesada gave Lieutenant Kohl a salute. "Our family is fortunate you survived. Prepare a complete report when your condition permits."

The broken and bleeding officer grasped at his uncle's hand. *"Comandante*, did you kill them?"

"We will," said Quesada. "Be certain of that. The fighting continues. Soon we will know. Now rest, be strong...." He leaned close to Lieutenant Kohl so that the others would not hear. "Your Fatherland and the New Reich need you."

The lieutenant balled his left fist against his chest,

then extended his arm out straight in a variation of the Nazi salute.

Colonel Quesada paced away from the dead and the suffering men. Outside, he saw the helicopter waiting in the center of the garden lawns. Captain Mendez shouted over the roar.

"There is shooting outside the west gate," he reported. "May I delay your departure while I take my squad to the fight?"

"No! We go on to Honduras. I do my duty to the Reich, before I take revenge on the attackers."

The colonel ran across the courtyards and garden walkways to the waiting helicopter. In moments, the Huey lifted away, carrying Colonel Quesada to the safety of the Honduran mountains.

19

A lightshow of death—red tracers, green tracers, the orange yellow flame slashes of RPG-7 rockets—streaked from the night-black hillside. Amazed by the intensity of the one-way firefight that would end their lives, Blancanales and Lyons and Ricardo stared at the flashing autofire, reflexes locking their hands on their weapons, their reason abandoning all hope. But not a bullet hit them. Their heads pivoted as their jeep sped through the kill zone.

Behind them, the storm of full-metal-jacketed slugs tore the two pursuing trucks to bloody junk. The Quesada militiamen, who chased Lyons and Blancanales and the teenager knew only an instant of the high-velocity maelstrom—headlights exploding, windshields shattering, windows dissolving into glitter, sheet-steel deforming—before falling into the endless night of death.

Tires popped. The first truck went into a sideskid across the wet pavement, the steering wheel in the hands of a dead man. Ten lines of tracers focused on the truck. An RPG's warhead hit. Metallic points of flame sprayed into the night, then petroflame engulfed the rolling hulk.

A rocket flashed from the hillside to hit the second truck. Ragged sheet steel spun into the low brush beyond the road. A fireball churned into the darkness and rain.

Blancanales glanced in the rearview mirror and saw only flames. Then a wall of headlights appeared in front of him. The shadowy forms of cars blocked the road.

Stomping the brakes, Blancanales fought the fishtailing jeep. He danced the pedals, downshifting, braking, downshifting again. Desperate for an escape route, he steered for the hillside's muddy embankment. He would go above the roadblock.

Gadgets Schwarz stepped into the glare of the headlights and waved his arms.

"What's happening here?" Blancanales wondered as he stood on the brake.

In pain, Lyons laughed. "Ask Mr. Wizard."

The jeep slid to a stop. Gadgets ran to his partners. He slapped Lyons on the back.

"Saw that stunt show through binocs!" he exclaimed. "Don't ever ask to borrow my car." He leaned across and jabbed Blancanales in the shoulder. "Wait till you see who's here. Floyd Jefferson! And some people from the other side...." He glanced to the darkness of the hillside and whispered, "Just be cool. They're on our side, tonight. I explained what we're doing and it's cool. Be cool."

"What are you talking about?" Lyons's eyes scanned the darkness as he reached for his Atchisson.

Gadgets's hand closed around his partner's wrist and moved his hand away from the autoshotgun. "Be cool, Ironman, or you'll be scrap metal. You're standing in the wrecking yard...."

Shadows came from the hillside. Against the flaming hulks of the militia trucks, they saw the silhouettes carrying an international collection of autoweapons. Israeli Galil rifles. M-60 machine guns. An M-14. Heckler & Koch G-3s. Two forms carried Soviet RPG launchers and slung CAR-15s.

"Hey specialists!" Floyd Jefferson called out. The young reporter from San Francisco, California, ran from the silhouettes. A camera on a strap bounced against his side. A shotgun bandolier loaded with 35mm film cans crossed his rain-soaked camouflage shirt.

Lyons shoulder-slung his Atchisson and got out of the jeep. He swayed on his feet. Floyd ran up and hugged his ex-cop friend.

"Easy, kid." Lyons winced with pain. "I just totaled a truck."

"Oh, yeah! Saw it. All the *muchachos* think you're *fantastico*. Ain't seen you since... since...."

"Since I carried you to that ambulance. How's your head?"

"Call me Fearless Fosdick. Thank God for my Irish skullbone. Had a concussion. But one in my ribs was the pits. Couldn't take a deep breath for nine weeks."

Blancanales walked around the jeep. He exchanged an *abrazo* with the Puerto Rican-Irish-Mexican-Indian-Anglo young man. Looking past Floyd, he asked quietly, "Who are they?"

Floyd turned. He saw the platoon of men in camou uniforms only steps away. He briefed Able Team quickly. "Democratic Liberation Front. Ex-Salvo soldiers and officers. They don't fight, they kill. You saw. They're specialists, just like you. Lizco will explain everything."

"The lieutenant's with them?" Lyons asked. "I thought so...."

"The other Lizco," Gadgets corrected.

The Lieutenant Lizco whom Lyons knew came from the headlights. He had his M-16 slung over one shoulder. He joined the guerrillas crowding around Able Team.

"I introduce my brother, Captain Alfredo Lizco," he said.

His older brother extended a hand to Lyons and Blancanales. "Pleased to meet you. Enemies of Quesada are my friends."

"Mucho gusto, comrade," Blancanales said.

"Amigo," the captain corrected. "That other word is for other fighters."

"You're not Communists?" Lyons asked, shaking the captain's hand with enthusiasm.

"No!" The older Lizco spat out the denial. "Now come. We talk too much here."

Slowly, painfully, Lyons stepped back into the jeep. Captain Lizco caught his arm.

"Please," he said. "Come with us in truck. We talk in truck."

"Are we your prisoners?" Lyons asked.

"We do not take prisoners," the captain stated simply.

Gadgets laughed. "The man talks straight. In the truck, Ironman. We got to make out of here, *muy rápido*."

Two guerrillas got in the jeep. Pausing to find only empty Atchisson mags on the floor of the jeep, Lyons followed the others. He staggered a few steps to catch up with Guillermo Lizco, the lieutenant.

"Why didn't you say your big brother was up here?" he said. "Me and my partner and Ricardo just took the kamikaze tour of the Quesada estate. With two M-60s, we ripped that place apart. But with your brother's men, we could have taken Quesada and the plantation and all his people."

"Until an hour ago," the lieutenant answered, "I did not know my brother still lived."

"You just bumped into him? By coincidence?"

"No," the elder brother told him. Captain Lizco explained as they climbed into the back of a slat-side farm truck. "My commander send me here because my brother fights with Las Boinas Negras. I come to make contact with him. To stop the Stalinistas, those crazy Soviet *rojos* who kill everyone. Farmers, soldiers, children."

Able Team, the Lizco brothers and several guerrillas crowded into the truck. They had only plastic tarps to shelter them from the rain and the wind. The convoy of the truck and the two jeeps sped away from the burning hulks.

Guerrillas stuck the barrels of their autorifles and M-60 machine guns out the slats. One machine gunner watched each side of the road. A rocketman slipped a projectile into his RPG launcher and straightened the wire on the rocket's safety cap.

"You killed the Stalinistas," Captain Lizco continued. "But still there are many questions. The people tell us of soldiers and Communist assassins together. Many strange stories. Now we will not know the truth about the Communists and what they did. But I thank you for doing our work."

Lyons looked to Blancanales and Ricardo, cautioning them to silence. "But the Communists are your allies. Why would you want them dead?"

"There are Communists, yes, in our alliance. There are Marxists, there are Socialists. Unionists, Christian Democrats, Indians, Jews, Buddhists, anarchists, utopians. There are many ideologies. But they do not slaughter campesinos and their families. They do not kill every thing that lives. What the Stalinistas do is a crime against God. They are not our allies, they are not fighting for Salvador. They fight only to take. Like the Soviets. The Soviets are not Communists. They want only power. Communist, Soviet, Stalinist, fascist, Nazi. Only words. They are the same. They are terrormongers for power.''

Lyons laughed. ''That is the fact. You, sir, know an international truth. The kid there—'' he pointed to Ricardo ''—he was with the PLF. We wiped out the Commie unit, but we didn't get their officer. When we infiltrated the plantation, Ricardo spotted his officer with the fascists—''

''What?'' the captain asked.

''We saw La Víbora,'' Blancanales repeated.

''Mr. Snake,'' Lyons continued. ''With a Salvadoran army officer. On their way to meet with that Nazi Colonel Quesada.''

''And I called you paranoid,'' Gadgets commented to Lyons. ''Maybe I don't have the imagination for Salvadoran politics.''

''Who could?'' Lyons answered.

''This La Víbora,'' the captain asked, ''he is still with Quesada?''

''He's dead. Ricardo killed him with a frag.''

''That is a problem,'' the captain said. ''Many questions will not be answered. We will not learn who else collaborates with the families.''

''Ask Quesada,'' Lyons told him.

Blancanales shook his head. ''The mission's over. Like you said, we lost the element of surprise. Now he knows we're here.''

''He knew we were here—'' Gadgets spoke up.

Lyons interrupted. ''He thinks some mercenaries rescued a squad of soldiers. He still doesn't know who hit him and why.''

''Ironman, Quesada Nazado knows!'' insisted Gadgets. ''That's why he canceled the ambush of the journalists. The death-squad officer wanted to go find the reporters. But Quesada told him there were, and I quote, 'North American agents sent to kidnap him.' He wanted the officer, a Lieutenant Kohl, to attend a meeting. I got that right, Lieutenant?''

The younger Lizco brother made a correction. "He said you were 'North American paramilitary agents.' ''

"I knew it!" Lyons cursed. "I knew it. That's why I won't use Agency papers. That's why I didn't trust the lieutenant here. We can't even trust our own government."

"Not the government," Blancanales told him. "Individuals within the government. Or the administration. Or Congress. Or the Agency. Somewhere, there's someone working for the Salvadoran fascists. Someone with access to our mission information. Before the next mission, we'll have to deal with the informer."

Lyons shook his head no. "We're not going back without the Man. We'll ask him who the informer is. He'll know."

"I vote for a tactical withdrawal," Blancanales stated. "They know we're here. They know we're after Quesada. The *finca* will be locked down so tight it'd take a battalion of Marines to seize him. And you, we have to get you to a hospital for a few days' observation."

"I'm all right!" Lyons said.

"You hit that gate at eighty or ninety miles an hour. You could have a subdural hematoma. You could have a ruptured spleen. You could have a hundred internal hemorrhages. You could fall over dead any minute. Soon as the Wizard can put out the signal, we're on our way back."

"Hard to argue with that," Gadgets told Lyons. "Second the motion. Don't want to lose our shock-trooper."

"Captain—" Lyons turned to the guerrilla officer "—Quesada's in that plantation. He has the answers to your questions. You want to go get that Nazi, I'll go with you."

The captain smiled. He looked to his younger brother. "Who are these men you brought to our country? They kill the Stalinists, they kill the fascists. Other North Americans talk of democracy, but they—" he pointed at the three warriors of Able Team "—they fight for democracy."

The brothers laughed. The captain turned to his men and translated what had been said. Some laughed. Others gave Lyons the clenched-fist salute. One man talked with his leader for a moment. The captain turned to Able Team again.

"That man says to remember the Abraham Lincoln Brigade in Spain. When the Spanish people fought the Castilian fascists and the German Nazis, some North Americans joined the war. Perhaps if an Abraham Lincoln Brigade came to Salvador, we could make a democracy."

"Captain," Lyons told him, "what you want for your country is your business. I'm fighting for my country. To protect my country's democracy. There are Nazis threatening my country and Quesada knows who they are. I want to put the question to that fascist scumhole. It is a personal mission. I'm out for revenge and he is the first step. So what is it? Do we go in?"

"Hey, Ironman," Gadgets broke in. "You are exceeding your authority."

Blancanales spoke in a low voice. "You are not for revenge. Our mission here is to return Quesada for trial."

"Okay!" Lyons snapped. "There it is. That's our mission. We'll do it. Stop this tactical retreat talk. So what if he knows we're coming?"

The truck's driver called back to his captain. *"Aquí está el carro de los norteamericanos."*

"Your other jeep," Captain Lizco told them.

Two riflemen in black plastic ponchos left the cover of roadside brush when they saw their unit returning.

Blancanales called across the truck. "Floyd!" The young reporter had listened to the debate, quietly translating details for the Salvadorans. "You're college educated. You're in this. What do you say?" Blancanales asked him.

"Rick Marquez got me my first job. Without him, I'd still be a punk with a camera looking for work. And Quesada had him murdered. So don't expect me to say anything. . .anything moderate. I say nuke Quesada."

Gadgets ran back to the waiting truck. "Political! Things have changed! I set my gear to monitor and record and what did I catch? Quesada's gone to someplace called Reitoca, in Honduras. To something called 'The School.' He ain't hiding inside the plantation, and he won't expect us to hit him in Honduras. What do you say?"

Lyons did not wait for Blancanales to answer Schwarz. The blond ex-cop turned to the Salvadorans.

"Where is Reitoca? How far? And can we get there tonight?"

20

Jack Grimaldi had landed in Tegucigalpa in the darkness and wind-driven rain of the storm from the Pacific. After a leisurely meal of reheated Air Force lasagna and stale white bread, downed with a six-pack of Honduran beer, he borrowed a raincoat and went to examine the men and aircraft available for his latest Stony Man assignment.

Sometime in the next three to seven days, Able Team would radio him for a lift out of El Salvador. Maybe they would radio from an airfield. Maybe they would radio from a clearing in the mountains. He needed mechanically dependable aircraft available twenty-four hours a day, with standby personnel to service the aircraft and man the flights.

At the military end of the airfield, the Central Intelligence Agency maintained a secret air force. An officer in the Agency's Langley offices had agreed over the phone to furnish a helicopter or plane for the Able Team mission. But an Agency promise in Washington, D.C., did not mean a plane and crew in Tegucigalpa.

Interdepartmental rivalries! Grimaldi walked through the rain cursing the problems created by petty bureaucratic egotism. Army Intelligence won't help Navy Intelligence. The Air Force won't help the NSA. The State Department wages paper wars with the National Security Council. Fight the Reds, fight terrorism, fight Libya, maybe the Frenchies, too. But first, we fight each other.

Likely as not, they'll tell me to type up an official request and send it to my congressman.

Continuing to the lighted window of a hangar's office, Grimaldi tried the door. Locked. He knocked. No answer. He knocked on the window. Condensation on the glass allowed him only a fuzzy view of the interior. After he pounded on the sheet-steel door with his fist, a face appeared at the window.

"Who's that out there?" a voice shouted.

"The name's Jack Eagle. You got a cable about me."

The door opened. A tall, bearded man with T-shirt bulging over a beer belly motioned him inside. "Been waiting all day for you, Jack. They buzzed us from up north that you'd be doing some taxi work."

"Here's my identification." Grimaldi displayed authorization papers complete with signatures and carbon copies.

"Well, yeah. Those look good. Got the right John Hancock down there. Recognize the name. Not that papers mean shit. You can call me Tennessee, Jack."

"Thanks for the cooperation, Tennessee. I need to take a trip into the mountains."

The other man laughed. "Yeah, that's what we do here. In fact, that's all we do. Question is, fixed wing or rotor?"

"Both, whatever—"

"We don't have any of those!" Laughing again, Tennessee led him through the office and into the hangar. "Least, not this week."

"I mean, I won't know until I get the signal. I'll need a standby helicopter and a standby plane. And personnel."

"Daylight or night pickup?"

In the dark interior of the hangar, Grimaldi saw a war-surplus Huey painted with midnight-blue enamel and corporate logos. Bullet holes pocked the panels. Beyond that helicopter, other Hueys waited in various stages of maintenance. Masking tape and gray primer paint covered the side of one helicopter.

"Twenty-four-hour standby," Grimaldi said.

"Hot or cold?"

Grimaldi glanced at the maintenance logs on the midnight-blue "corporate shuttle" helicopter. He compared the air hours to the dates of the service. "What do you mean?"

"The LZ."

"Won't know until I get the signal. In fact, it could change by the time I get to the landing zone."

"How many passengers returning? And what's the approximate weight of returning equipment?"

"Three for sure. Maybe two others. And hand luggage."

"Those numbers are subject to cancellation, right? We get calls to take out ten passengers. We show up, and three and four have been 'canceled' by the time we get there."

"No cancellations possible. I hope."

"We don't deal in hopes. We deal in lift weight. But if you're talking helicopters, five men or one man, it don't make that much difference. All we got is Hueys. But in planes, it means something."

The maintenance records of the blue Huey indicated the mechanics had dedicated themselves to keeping the helicopter airborne. Routine work exceeded requirements. When one hydraulic hose showed a crack, the mechanics replaced all the hoses and refilled the system with new fluid. Mechanics replaced control cables before even one strand frayed.

"I want this one," Grimaldi told Tennessee.

"Don't you want to wait on the bodywork?" Tennessee pointed to the bullet holes. "Isn't it amazing what birds can do to aluminum? Fly into an aircraft, punch their little beaks through the sheet metal. Sure messed up the company paint job. You'd think it was deliberate."

The Stony Man flier put the tip of his finger into one dent. "Seven-point-six-two-millimeter beaks. The birds must be Kalashnikov snow storks. Didn't think their migratory patterns took them through Central America."

The Agency man laughed. "Pesky critters. Flying around everywhere these days."

"The birds get to any of the workings?"

"No mechanical damage whatsoever, sir. No, sir. Would've fixed that first. We worry about sheet metal and paint last around here. But while you're waiting for your passenger signal, we'll do the touch-ups."

"And what other equipment can I requisition? Like some guns for the doors. To keep those snow storks back."

"M-60s do? Got mini-Gatlings. Or 40mm machine guns. Those Gatlings put down a flock at a time."

"Interesting. What happens if I need additional equipment and aircraft? Maybe my people will need some kind of backup."

"Whatever you want, Mister Eagle. We got it all. Personnel on one-hour call. Give us a ring, we wake them up."

The pager at Grimaldi's belt buzzed. The signal meant the ultra-high-frequency radio in his plane had received a burst transmission. The transmission meant something had gone wrong.

Fifteen minutes later, Grimaldi piloted the midnight-blue Huey into the storm.

21

All the Democratic Front fighters volunteered to join in the assault on the fascist stronghold in the Honduran mountains. But the Huey could carry only the weight of fourteen men and their weapons. The former Salvadoran army officers and soldiers drew lots to determine who would accompany the North Americans across the Honduran border.

A plastic tarp sheltering them from the drizzling rain, Able Team went through all their weapons and equipment by the light of an electric lantern. The three North Americans took only what they needed for the assault. Their suitcases, backpacks, rations and field equipment would remain with the Democratic Front fighters who stayed behind.

"You know what happens if the politicians ever find out about this?" Gadgets asked his partners. "Foreign policy nightmare."

"About what?" Lyons asked. "Us killing fascists? You got it. Hope it starts an international fad."

"No! This stuff. We're giving it to guerrillas. Even if they aren't Commies, they're antigovernment."

"We need their help," Lyons said. "If Quesada ran off to someplace safe, I figure that place will have more defenses than his plantation did."

"Elementary, my dear Ironman. They teach you to think like that in college?" Gadgets countered. "But think about this. We're donating this gear to the guerrillas. The guerrillas are fighting the government of El Salvador. The government of El Salvador is a regional ally of the United States—"

"No ally of mine! How many U.S. citizens have the Salvos murdered so far? Nuns, social workers, lawyers, reporters, tourists! All the killers were army or national guard. Any of those goons go to trial? Captain Lizco says his men specialize in wiping out death squads. I don't mind helping his people, not at all. Wish I could donate a ton of ammunition."

"Ironman the hardcore diplomat," Gadgets said, laughing. "You make it simple."

"What's difficult? Kill an American, die."

A voice called out from the crowd of Democratic Front fighters. "Hey specialists!"

Floyd Jefferson splashed through the muddy water flowing down the hillsides. "Those guys say eight of them are going in the helicopter. Counting you three and the lieutenant, his brother and the teenager, that doesn't leave room for me. You cutting out the press coverage of this revolutionary event?"

"No room for the press corps," Gadgets told him. "Besides, you can't take pictures in the dark."

"I can write a story."

Lyons groaned. "Just what we need. I can see the headline. 'U.S. Paramilitary Agents and Communist Terrorists Attack Convention of Salvadoran Businessmen.' "

"How 'bout this one. 'Justice in the Night! Freedom Fighters Annihilate Nazis!' " Floyd said.

Lyons laughed. "Sounds good. Good enough to get us into a congressional investigation. Here's another headline. 'Freedom Fighters Rot in Leavenworth.' "

"Okay, no story," Floyd told them. "But I got to go. I've spent the past few months working on this. Checking out every Nazi group in the Americas. The Argentinian, the Chileans, the Salvadorans, the North American gangs. All of the groups. I made contact with the Democratic Front so that I could join their group here to check out Quesada. We know Quesada's one of them. Now he's run off to someplace named The School. I want to go. Maybe La Escuela is just one more *finca* in the mountains. But maybe it isn't. Look at the map...."

The young reporter spread out a map of El Salvador, Honduras and Nicaragua. "Here's the Contra war zone in northern Nicaragua. There are reports of Argentinians working with the Somoza gangs. Here's El Salvador. I've spotted blond guys working with the national-guard death squads. They talked Spanish but they weren't Salvos. A report came out of Honduras of death squads led by Chilean secret police. Now here's Reitoca. If you had an international operation going, wouldn't you put the headquarters in a central location?"

The three men of Able Team glanced to one another. They knew much more about Nazis than Floyd. They had fought the conspiracy of Unomundo to seize Guatemala with an army of Guatemalan traitors and Salvadoran fascists and foreign mercenaries. They had seen Salvadoran fascists at parties with United States lawmakers. And now, Quesada had escaped because of a traitor in the United States government.

Careful not to betray his own knowledge, Blancanales questioned Floyd. "You think there's a Pan-American Nazi movement?"

"That's what I think."

"Couldn't your Nazi conspiracy just be right wingers cooperating with one another?"

"I think it's more than that. In Argentina and Chile

and Bolivia, there are Nazi communities. They march around behind the swastika, do the 'Sieg Heil' boogie. In Argentina, the army keeps pictures of Hitler in the barracks. In El Salvador, you ever seen the salute of the Arena Party?''

Floyd snapped his right fist to the center of his chest, then shot out his arm in a Nazi salute.

''There it is. That's what goes on. Even in the U.S. of A., things are weird.''

''What do you mean?'' Blancanales continued his questioning.

''Like how Quesada skipped Miami. The FBI waited twenty-four hours after they got the warrant before they actually went to his mansion in North Beach. And the other Salvadorans who've murdered Americans—they've got condos and cars and businesses in Miami. Makes you think they got friends in high places.''

Lyons shook his head. ''It's going to be fourteen of us against whoever we find. Everybody who goes carries a weapon.''

''I can pull a trigger,'' Floyd insisted. ''I'll take an M-16.''

Lyons looked to his partners. ''What's the vote?''

Blancanales nodded. ''Floyd speaks English and Spanish. We could use him.''

''Talks jive, too.'' Gadgets grinned. ''I need a translator.''

''Go work it out with them.'' Lyons pointed at the men of the Democratic Front.

''All right!'' Floyd splashed away.

Gadgets laughed. ''The Ironman authorizes press coverage of a Team event. This is a first.''

''And a last,'' Lyons muttered.

The high-frequency radio clicked with a coded message. Gadgets listened, then translated as he grabbed flares and flashlights.

"Jack will be here in a minute. Time to guide him in."

THE HUEY BUCKED through clouds and mountain winds. Crowded into the interior, the fourteen men sat shoulder to shoulder on the seats and on the floor. Autoweapons, ammunition, rockets tangled with the men. Floyd Jefferson flashed portraits of the guerrillas sitting quiet and thoughtful among their laughing and shouting compatriots.

Only a few seconds after they left the Morazan hillside behind, the intercom buzzed. Grimaldi, alone in the pilot's cabin, asked Able Team, "Hey, ah. . . what goes on? Who are those troopers with you?"

Gadgets passed the headset to Blancanales. "You explain this."

"Not me." Blancanales passed the headset to Lyons.

Pressing through the mass of men and weapons, Lyons leaned forward to Grimaldi. Behind him a camera flashed. He shouted back, "No photos!"

Floyd responded. "Not taking pictures of you. Of the other guys."

"Interesting group of soldiers," Grimaldi said over his shoulder.

"Irregulars," Lyons told him.

"Uh-huh. Mercenaries?"

"No. But they're hot. They can pop hundred percent kill count ambushes."

"What do the initials DFL mean?"

"Democratic Front for the Liberation."

"Oh, shit, man. What are you doing? Are you involved in some kind of guerrilla action?"

"These guys aren't Reds," Lyons replied. "They're

ex-army. Some of them were trained at Fort Bragg. Their officer was a captain in the army, a LRRP. He got involved in the land reforms. The Nazis sent a death squad, so he went to the mountains. I would've done the same thing.''

Though he kept his promise of never showing the faces of Able Team, Floyd Jefferson allowed their nightsuits and weapons to appear in the photo frames. The high-quality uniforms and web-gear contrasted with the patched and hand-sewn uniforms of the Democratic Front fighters. The immaculate, high-tech weapons of the North Americans appeared behind the scarred and worry-lined faces of men who now fought against the government that the United States financed and armed. Every shot of the men had the background of the Huey panels and the rain-beaded Plexiglas side windows.

"Able Team's got the reputation for the weirdest, but this is the limit, you know that?'' continued Grimaldi. "Do you realize these guerrillas are the enemies of your country? This is just totally—''

Lyons shouted down the Stony Man flier. "One, there has been no declaration of war, therefore they are not the enemies of my country. Two, whatever goes on between them and their government, I don't care. That's Salvadoran politics. And wait until you get the debriefing report on this mission—compared to the scum-snakes we found down there, these guys are Boy Scouts. Three, we need fighters and they volunteered. Four, you're paid to fly. So fly.''

"You got the exact location of this school?''

"We'll find it. There'll be an airfield and two helicopters. Lights. A perimeter. If we don't see it on the flyby, we'll get out and look for it.''

"Then what?''

"Any chance you can come back with a B-52?"

"You serious? You want them bombed?"

"First we need to take Quesada alive. But then we'll waste the place. How can you help us?"

"The Agency's got cargo planes—"

"The Agency? Forget it. There's Nazi informers operating in the Agency. Quesada got warned we were coming. We've been betrayed by someone in the Agency or in the administration."

"I don't want to hear that talk! Running around with guerrillas, now you're sounding like a Commie."

"I'm talking the facts."

"Hear this, crazyman. The Agency gave me total co-operation. I was very pleasantly surprised."

"Be ready for unpleasant surprises. You tell them where you were going with this helicopter?"

"Never tell anybody anything."

"Don't tell them where you take the bomber."

"I don't know about bombs," Grimaldi said, shaking his head. "Especially on short notice."

"Improvise," Lyons said. "Use your imagination. We need maximum effect. Otherwise we'll have a Nazi army chewing at us through the mountains."

Grimaldi pointed down. "We're over the coordinates of that town."

"Stay high. Circle out. I'll be sitting in the door looking out."

Lyons motioned to his partners. He went to a door and buckled on the safety straps. Cautioning the men around him, he eased the door open.

Cold night wind and rotor-whipped rain struck him. Thousands of feet below, he saw darkness and the tiny points of lights. But no patterns of lights. He scanned the depthless black of the unseen mountains for La Escuela. Gadgets's voice spoke through the intercom.

"Bear to the left...."

"Yeah, I see the lights," Grimaldi answered. "I'll take you past."

"What you see?" Lyons asked his partner in the other door.

"Airstrip lights. And the landing lights of a plane. Man, that is an installation."

The fighters turned to stare out at a mountaintop crowned with brilliant points. A rectangle of blue dots framed an asphalt runway. As they watched, a plane descended from the night, cones of white glare projecting from the wings.

When the plane taxied to a stop, the landing lights and the runway lights switched off. The blue rectangle faded to darkness.

A ring of white security lights remained on the mountain. Scattered points of incandescent glow indicated buildings. The scene wheeled into view as the helicopter continued in a slow circle. Grimaldi spoke through the intercom.

"That's the place you want me to bomb?"

"Don't look like there's anyplace else," Gadgets answered. "But we'll check it out."

"Put us down," Lyons told the flier. "And when you come back, come loaded."

22

Jon Gunther, chief of personal security for Klaust de la Unomundo-Stiglitz, listened with interest to the ravings of Colonel Roberto Quesada. The Salvadoran spoke with anger and bravado, yet Gunther knew the colonel lied.

In preparation for a conference of Central American military and political men loyal to Unomundo's International Alliance, Gunther and his aides had flown to La Escuela to review the staff's security procedures. Now, only minutes after their arrival, Gunther knew he must cancel the conference. To do otherwise—to accept the assurances of The School officers, to accept the pompous delusions of the colonel—would be to expose his leader to danger.

Colonel Quesada, his tailored fatigues soaked, paced the conference hall, motioning with his clenched fist for dramatic emphasis. He told a story of his soldiers betrayed and murdered in the United States. A Negro assassin impersonating a leftist journalist had lured his soldiers into an ambush on a residential street in San Francisco, California. North American mercenaries then lured two squads of his soldiers into death traps in the mountains of California and the slums of Los Angeles. Only with the help of Internationalists in the U.S. government had Quesada escaped a ridiculous arrest warrant issued by the United States Department of Justice.

But the mercenaries had relentlessly pursued him to
El Salvador. There, this night, under the cover of the
unnatural storm from the Pacific, forces led by North
American commandos mounted suicide attacks on the
defenses of La Finca Quesada. Despite his personal
leadership in the firefights, the invaders breached the
outer defenses, only to die, Quesada insisted, in heaps at
the walls of the family's residence. He had left the
counterattack on the fleeing cowards to his junior officers.

Despite the threats against his family and his proper-
ties, the colonel flew on to La Escuela. He knew his re-
sponsibility to the International Alliance. He would
represent the Quesada family at the conference. Quesada paused in his long story, then delivered his declaration.

"The Fourteen Families of El Salvador, united in
patriotism and courage, will join the leaders of the other
nations of the Americas in the hemispheric victory of
the International Alliance!" He snapped his fist to his
chest, then extended his straightened hand and arm.

"Victory to the New Reich!"

Gunther restrained his laughter. Throughout the
pompous colonel's speech, the security chief had men-
tally noted the lies.

"The Negro assassin impersonating a journalist"
had, in fact, been a journalist. Floyd Jefferson, a
twenty-two-year-old leftist with no military experience,
had confronted and killed two of the four soldiers sent
to kidnap him.

The mercenaries who "lured" Quesada's soldiers into
death traps had demonstrated only basic military techniques. In the first "death trap," Quesada's death squad
pursued the North Americans from the interstate highway. The North Americans turned off a road and

waited in a narrow canyon. In complete disregard of caution, the death squad's three trucks drove into the ambush. In the second "death trap," the North Americans attacked the Salvadorans as they stood in a group in the center of a Los Angeles street.

Death traps? No. Only arrogant and stupid soldiers meeting death in a confrontation with intelligent, disciplined fighters.

But the assault on the *finca* worried Gunther. On the eve of what would have been his leader's seizure of Guatemala, North Americans had infiltrated and destroyed the secret base of the army of Unomundo high in the Sierra de Cuchumantes. The assault had come virtually without warning: no firefights, no attacks on the perimeters; only an all-consuming ball of flame that killed a thousand soldiers in their barracks. A squad of Quiche Indians led by North American commandos had liquidated the survivors in a brief small-arms assault. By luck, Gunther had been airborne in a helicopter at the time of the attack. Of more than a thousand soldiers, assassins, officers, technicians and pilots, only Unomundo and Gunther and three soldiers plus the helicopter's pilots survived.

The new attacks seemed similar. Gunther questioned the Salvadoran.

"Colonel Quesada, I am familiar with your estate's very impressive security perimeter. Fences, towers, mine fields. All the modern devices. Even in the darkness and rain, I do not understand how they overwhelmed your perimeter defenses."

"I await a report," replied Quesada. "I will share that information with you the moment I receive it."

"They gained entry without an alarm sounding?"

"We suspect they parachuted agents into the coffee fields."

"Could they have had agents in your security forces?"

"No! My men are loyal. They know the penalty for treason."

"When did the fighting first break out?"

"As they assaulted the walls of the family compound—"

"They passed through all your defenses, all your forces? You did not know of the attack until they rushed the walls?"

"They are very cunning. We will question the prisoners—"

"Yes, the prisoners. Did you not personally question them?"

"My duties required my presence here."

"How many prisoners did your men take?"

"I await a report on the action."

"How many Communists did your men kill?"

"Many! I will report on the numbers killed when I receive the report."

"Did you kill the North Americans?"

"Certainly. They could not have escaped our counterattack."

"Did you see the North Americans?"

"In the confusion of the battle, I saw only the fighting."

"But you said North Americans led the Communists."

"Yes. North Americans."

"How do you know if you did not see them?"

"One of my trusted lieutenants, they took him prisoner for a moment until he fought his way free. He saw their faces. One was blond. The other—"

"This lieutenant, I would like to question him."

"When his wounds allow an interview, I will summon him here."

"Good. I must return to give my report to our leader immediately."

The colonel protested. "But you have been here at the School only a few minutes."

"We leave the moment our jet is refueled."

Minutes later, the Lear jet streaked north on a nonstop return flight to Washington, D.C.

23

Engines whined, then the misting rain became blue. Gadgets Schwarz looked up to see a small jet lift away from the mountaintop, the airstrip's blue lights reflecting from the underside of the wings and fuselage. He took the moment of artificial moonlight to check his work.

In order to prevent the cutting of the perimeter fence by intruders, security technicians had woven filaments through the chain link. Electric charges pulsing through the filaments allowed guards to remotely monitor the perimeter.

Working by the digital readout of his own monitor, Gadgets had clipped "jumpers" to each filament. He quickly checked each of three filaments, the first just below the soil, the second about a foot off the ground, the third about two feet up the fence. With plastic ties, he secured the three jump lines in a semicircular arch.

The mountaintop lights went black. Gadgets paused for his eyes to readjust to the darkness. A hundred meters away, security lights created a soft glow in the sky. A searchlight on a mechanical mount swept the cleared ground in automatic cycles. Above the brilliant beam, the shadowy outline of a guard tower stood against the night.

Though the storm had died away to drizzle and intermittent downpours, a slow wind pushed low clouds over the mountain. From time to time, clouds made luminescent by the lights enveloped the hillsides. Other times, darkness returned.

Gadgets waited until the light swept past, then put his wire cutters to the filaments. He watched the digital numbers and snipped the three filaments. The cuts did not interrupt the pulses.

With heavier snips, he cut a shoulder-wide hole through the fence. He snapped his fingers to Lyons and Blancanales.

His partners joined him. In whispers, they compared observations.

"Mines." Lyons pointed to the patterns of depressions in the shaggy grass. The earth over the antipersonnel devices had settled, exposing the location of every mine.

"Those will be no problem," Blancanales commented. He turned to Gadgets. "Are there others?"

"I'll go first with the detector," Gadgets told them. "But if anybody wanders off my path, it's all over."

Blancanales slid back through the brush. He hissed to the Lizco brothers and motioned them forward. The two brothers—one on active duty with the government, one fighting the government—joined Able Team at the fence.

"There, mines." Blancanales pointed to the depressions in the no-man's-land.

Captain Lizco, the guerrilla officer, laughed softly. "I have seen it before. We have a man who is very good at this. He will lead us through."

"I've got a metal detector," Gadgets told the captain.

"Very good. You lead, my man will mark the path."

The captain crawled back to his men. Gadgets slipped a vinyl case from his backpack. He assembled components and flicked on the power switch of a small, hand-held unit. Passing it near the fence, it clicked.

"Ready to go."

Guerrillas took positions along the chain link fence. Unslinging their autorifles, they prepared to cover the infiltrators. Gadgets whispered to the nearest man.

"No lo toquen ustedes fusiles," he cautioned, pointing to the fence. The guerrilla nodded and passed the warning down the line. No one touched the fence with his rifles.

The men with Galils snapped down the bipods. The men who carried rocket launchers moved close to the hole in the fence. In case of detection and a withdrawal-under-fire by the infiltrators, the rocketmen would put RPG warheads into the guard towers.

A guerrilla scurried to the North Americans. Like Gadgets, the Salvadoran carried a CAR-15. But instead of electronics, the guerrilla carried a spool of string and a bundle of short, sharpened sticks. Gadgets took the string and examined it closely. The string gave off a faint blue glow.

"Oh, wow," he murmured to his partners. "Ain't seen this since Nam. The People's Army used string and wire to guide their squads to assembly points outside the perimeter. *¿Quien técha usted esto? Los Cubanos? Las Sandinistas?"*

"Un norteamericano de los Fuerzas Especiales," the guerrilla answered. *"Cuando yo fui en el ejercito."*

"No wonder these guys are good," Gadgets said. "The U.S. Special Forces trained them. *Vamos....*"

Gadgets led the way, waving the metal detector over the muddy earth. After knotting the string to the chain link, the guerrilla followed close behind the North American's boots. He jabbed a stick into the soil, then looped the string around the stick. The string marked the path through the mines.

The mechanical searchlight swept across the no-man's-land with the predictability of a lighthouse beam.

In the misting rain, Gadgets and the Salvadoran worked for a minute at a time, then went flat in the mud and weeds until the light passed over them. Soon, Lyons and Blancanales felt their hand-radios click.

Blancanales went first, following the glowing line of the string through the darkness. A few meters inside the fence, the path through the mines zigzagged, veering to the right, to the left, then to the right again. He saw the beam of the mechanical searchlight approaching.

He went flat. As the light swept over him, the diffuse glow illuminated the pattern of mines around him. He saw the shallow sinkhole of a mine only inches from his face. When the light passed, he continued, the line of faint light leading him quickly to another chain link fence.

Beyond the fence, they saw aircraft hangars. A concrete guardwalk curved away into the rain. The walkway crossed broken ground and lakes of muddy rainwater to circle the mountaintop. They saw no sentries pacing the areas between the hangars. From the guard tower fifty meters to the side, a radio played Latin dance rhythms.

Slipping out his Beretta, Blancanales covered Gadgets as he neutralized another line of electronic defense. Gadgets then left the guerrilla to cut the chain link while he went to another device.

In the gleam of the sweeping searchlight, Blancanales saw Gadgets snip wires, then jerk something from an upright pipe. Gadgets crept back to him.

"Guess what I got," he whispered, showing the flat object to his partner. "Might come in useful...."

Blancanales touched the object's casing. He read the raised letters with his fingertips: FRONT TOWARD ENEMY.

A claymore. Blancanales felt a cut piece of wire trailing from an electrical fuse. Gadgets went to disarm another of the electrically triggered antipersonnel weapons. Designed for the defense of perimeters, a claymore sprayed hundreds of steel pellets to saturate a fifty-meter kill zone.

Gadgets returned with the second claymore. Blancanales saw him slip it in a thigh pocket. He realized his partner carried a claymore in each of his nightsuit pants' thigh pockets.

"Get rid of those!" Blancanales hissed. "They're fused!"

"Throw this good stuff away?" Gadgets laughed softly. "I got plans for these."

Blancanales let Gadgets continue in his work. He scanned the walkway and the darkness, the Beretta ready, while Gadgets and the Salvadoran pulled out a rectangle of chain link.

First signaling Lyons and the others, they went through the inner fence. Blancanales went flat on asphalt and braced his Beretta in both hands. He watched the expanse of roads and runway for sentries. Gadgets faced the opposite direction, watching the walkway and the windows of the guard tower. Nothing moved.

Behind them, exploiting the periods of darkness between the sweeps of the searchlight, the squad negotiated the mine field. They slipped through the chain link and formed a wide half circle.

Lyons came last. Black clad, his gear smeared with mud and grass, the narrow band of his exposed skin darkened with grease, he looked like soil in motion. He pointed to himself and Blancanales, then to the tower.

Blancanales shook his head no. He pointed to the center of the mountaintop military base. Lyons crawled close to his Puerto Rican partner.

"Straight in?" he asked in a whisper.

Blancanales paused. "Except that we can't expect to

go out this way,'' he brooded. "This will probably be another Carl Lyons exit.''

"No more crashes tonight for me.''

"Are you okay?''

"I hurt. Oh, man, do I hurt.''

"Too late to medevac.''

"Did I ask for it?'' Lyons glanced to the lights of the buildings. "If we can't take Quesada out alive, we snuff him, right?''

"Can't put a dead man on trial,'' warned Blancanales.

"You actually think Washington would let it go that far?'' Lyons sneered. "He'd just get another ticket back to Salvador. The most I hope for is to put some questions to him. Everything else is dreaming. . . .''

Lyons slithered away, his silent auto-Colt in his right hand. He paralleled the walkway, his left shoulder to the concrete. The cast concrete stood a few inches above the mud. He stopped when the mechanical searchlight approached, pressing himself against the edge of the walkway, becoming only a shadow. He gained a hundred meters, the squad following in a line behind him. They left the aircraft area.

Ahead, Lyons saw another chain link fence. Topped with concertina wire, the fence separated the airstrip from the main area of buildings. Lights bathed the fence in daylight bright glare. On high poles, videocameras scanned the area.

Two guards patrolled the fence. At the far side of the asphalt, several hundred meters away from where the infiltrators lay in the mud and shadows, the guards walked the fence with a Doberman. Lyons keyed his hand-radio.

"No quiet way through this.''

"A diversion?'' Blancanales suggested.

Gadgets broke in. "You guys want a diversion? It means we can't go out through those holes in the fences."

"We decided a silent exit is unlikely," Blancanales whispered through the radio.

"Who decided? No one told me that. I got an electronic backup squad prepositioned back there."

"What do you mean?" Blancanales asked.

"You want a diversion? Yes or no? I'll make that guard tower...disappear!"

Lyons watched the sentries pace to the end of the fence. They turned. "Okay. Do it."

"Stand by for a big bang...." Gadgets laughed.

The Doberman barked. On the far side of the hangars, another dog barked. In seconds, dogs barked and wailed everywhere in the darkness.

Behind the squad of North Americans and Salvadorans, a second searchlight blazed from the guard tower. A guard swept the searing xenon beam along the outer perimeter.

A flash. The guard tower disintegrated in a spray of glass and wood and flesh. Where there had been lights and a tower, only darkness remained.

Sirens screamed. Headlights appeared on the far side of the airstrip. A Land Cruiser raced across the runway, spotlights on its roof revolving to illuminate the darkness in slow circles.

Other headlights stopped at the interior security fence. A remote-controlled gate rolled aside for an open truck crowded with soldiers. Some wore yellow raincoats, other black slickers. Others wore only gray fatigues. One man stood on the passenger-side cab step. Holding on to the door, he buckled on web-gear as the truck raced to the attack.

Lyons braced his silenced auto-Colt in both hands.

He sighted on the nearest of two videocameras surveilling the gate. As the truck accelerated through the gate, Lyons squeezed off a shot. He heard the slug skip off the camera housing and whine into the night. He adjusted his aim, fired again. The slug smashed the camera. Then he destroyed the second camera.

Sighting on the electric motor controlling gate, Lyons smashed it again and again with slugs. The gate jammed open. He keyed his hand-radio.

"Politico! The lights with your Beretta."

A light went dark. One by one, the nearest lights broke. Lyons heard tires squeal on asphalt. He turned to see the Land Cruiser and troop truck brake to a stop at the hole in the fence. Gray uniformed soldiers crowded from the truck.

Then a flash wiped them away. The battered, windowless hulks of the Land Cruiser and the truck rocked on their springs, surrounded by ruptured, smoldering flesh. Screams rose from the dismembered.

Blancanales sighted his M-16/M-203 and fired a high-explosive 40mm frag. The shell popped in the midst of the wreckage, gasoline flashing. The fireball rose into the darkness.

Lyons shouted out, "The gate!"

Other voices shouted in Spanish. Moving in one rush, the fourteen men sprinted through the flame-lit night.

24

Dropping down through the clouds in the borrowed DC-3, Grimaldi saw the flames. He eased into a wide circle around the mountaintop and watched the desperate firefight. From three thousand feet, he could see only the flashes of grenades and rockets. Streams of tracers streaked through the darkness. But he knew how many men—Able Team and their allies-of-expedience—he had dropped on a Honduran pasture. Those men now fought hundreds. When he returned with the Huey, he knew he would not take fourteen men out.

Grimaldi unplugged his headset. He slipped off the headphones and spoke into a Stony Man hand-radio.

"Able Team, this is the Eagle. Able Team , this is the Eagle. I'm up here with a surprise. Able Team, this is the—"

Lyons answered. Noise and autofire almost drowned out his voice. "What took you so long?"

Grimaldi glanced back to the cabin door before speaking again. No one had entered the pilot's cabin. "I got Agency people with me. They think we're over Ocotal, Nicaragua. How's it going?"

"Not too good. Had to shoot our way in. Still haven't found our man."

"Find him quick. I'm up here with five thousand liters of av-gas high-octane in plastic bladders. Give me a target. Won't make any bangs, but believe me, that place is going to be gone!"

"Stand by," Lyons told him. "We got to get organized. Over."

Replacing his headset, Grimaldi spoke into the intercom. "Gentlemen, prepare to crisp those Commie critters."

ON HIS BACK behind the concrete foundation of a prefab barrack, Lyons hooked his hand-radio onto his web belt. Autofire continued from the offices across the wide asphalt traffic circle. A Toyota Land Cruiser sat on its rims, its tires shot flat, its windows shot out, the bullet-ripped bodies of the soldiers jerking as crisscrossing autofire from both sides of the lane smashed it again and again.

The School had been constructed around the central lane. Branching out from the center lane, side streets led to auditoriums and classrooms and service buildings. In the center, offices clustered around the traffic circle. Beyond the offices, rows of barracks occupied the other half of the mountaintop.

Fighting past the classrooms, the squad of North Americans and Salvadorans met the concentrated fire of hundreds of gray-uniformed soldiers pouring from the barracks. The surprise attack had killed scores of the surprised soldiers, but the attack had failed. Alerted by the airfield alarm, the fascist officers had gathered their troops to annihilate the few infiltrators.

Now, NATO-caliber slugs from G-3 rifles and M-60 machine guns smashed through the plywood-and-aluminum wall only inches above Lyons's face. He felt the slap of slugs impacting the concrete foundation. Staying flat, he snaked along the foundation to Blancanales.

The Puerto Rican ex-Green Beret, working flat on his belly, taped a field dressing to a Salvadoran's bullet-smashed ribs. He spoke loud encouragement to the guerrilla as he worked to tape the man's arm against his torso. Lyons shouted to be heard.

"The Eagle's up there! He's got a thousand-something gallons of aviation gas in fuel bladders to drop."

Blancanales raged with anger. "Don't even *think* about another assault on those offices! He won't have any accuracy! We can't expect any kind of control. Grimaldi will burn us alive with that gas. You understand! Mister John Wayne hero motherfucker and your goddamned revenge!"

"Ease off," Lyons answered. He had never seen Blancanales this angry before. "I hereby vote for a withdrawal. No more of this, we're up against hundreds of them."

"What? Lyons the Brave recognizes a limit? *¡Gracias a Dios!*"

"Really, this is too much. Pass the word. The Eagle will drop that gas to cover the retreat. How's this Salvo?"

"Shattered ribs. Maybe bone fragments in his lung. But he can move. I'll pass the word to the others."

Blancanales spoke quickly to the wounded man, then went to Floyd. The two men spread word to the others. The survivors of the squad began a staggered retreat.

Lyons understood that he could not hope to search the base for Quesada. His bravado and daring had failed. He no longer thought of revenge, or of tearing information out of Quesada. He thought of getting his partners and friends out alive.

Counting by touch the Atchisson magazines in his bandolier, he found only three. Twenty-one rounds, plus three in his autoshotgun. He checked the setting of his fire-selector. Semiauto. Gripping the weapon, he joined the retreat.

He crabbed to the corner of the office building's foundation. A bloody Salvadoran with a Galil aimed single shots at the flashing muzzles of fascists across the street. But Lyons knew the lightweight 5.56mm slugs from the Galil might not penetrate the walls of the prefabs. Not like the 7.62 NATO slugs punching through the building above them.

Blancanales and Captain Lizco gathered their men. Scattered riflemen abandoned isolated positions. Darting from one building to another, throwing themselves flat behind the cover of the concrete foundations, the fighters assembled to continue the retreat.

Blancanales loaded one of his last 40mm shells. He aimed carefully at a window across the traffic circle. Captain Lizco braced his Galil, then shouted to his men.

The 40mm grenade flew through the window as the captain sprayed slugs through another window. The flash silhouetted fascists firing from inside. The firing stopped instantly as spring-steel shrapnel killed the fascists. The Salvadorans sprinted across the open ground.

Firing from other enemy positions now doubled. The prefab wall above the crawling men exploded with slugs and splintering wood. A rifle grenade burst in front of the building. Captain Lizco moved his men to the other end.

Lyons saw the men gathering behind him. He pointed out one window to the Salvadoran beside him, then pointed to himself and pointed to a second window. The Salvadoran nodded. Captain Lizco shouted out the signal.

The group bolted across the space. Lyons triggered quick semiauto blasts, punching steel shot into the faces of fascist gunners as the Salvadoran sprayed out a magazine of light 5.56mm slugs into other gunners.

All of the Salvadorans and North Americans made

the dash untouched. They fired at the fascist line of autoweapons as Lyons and the remaining Salvadoran made their run.

Grimaldi radioed again from the DC-3 circling overhead. "Give me a call, you crazies! You can't do it all yourself."

"We got to break out," Lyons answered. "We got wounded. We're up against hundreds of them. And they ain't just goons with guns. We busted into a military base."

"Mark their position! I'll heat up the situation."

"Okay, I'll mark it with a burning car. Stand by.... "

Blancanales listened in on his radio. Lyons pointed for Blancanales and Gadgets to continue. Then Lyons reloaded his Atchisson with slugs.

Gadgets shouted into his hand-radio, "Do it right, wingwipe. We're in the shit so deep we need a periscope."

The squad had the cover of a building for their withdrawal. Three riflemen directed fire at the offices and barracks to keep pursuers back as the squad crept backward.

Bolting to his feet, Lyons ran to the other end of the building. He eased around the corner. A dead fascist sprawled against the wall, his G-3 still locked in his hands.

Lyons set the safety on his Atchisson. Slinging the weapon over his shoulder, he stripped the man of his heavy-caliber rifle and bandolier of ammunition. On the soldier's web belt, he found a walkie-talkie and three rifle grenades. Though he had weapons, the attack on the base had surprised the soldier in the barracks. He wore gray fatigue pants and a silk pajama shirt.

Fitting a grenade to the muzzle of the G-3, Lyons aimed at the wrecked Land Cruiser and fired. The grenade smashed through the shattered rear window and bounced off the inside of the windshield. But Lyons heard no explosion. No gasoline flashed. A dud?

Searing white light illuminated the interior of the Land Cruiser. It had not been a grenade, but a flare. Lyons slipped another flare on the muzzle.

Behind him, the last Salvadorans withdrew. Alone against the massed rifles and machine guns of the hundreds of fascist soldiers, Lyons sighted the G-3's flare.

But the fascists had spotted him. A thousand slugs ripped the building. Lyons went flat, the grenade still in place as the building disintegrated above him. He heard shouts rallying the fascists.

He kicked the soldier's corpse into the open. Autofire destroyed it, dissolving the corpse in a pale spray of chopped flesh. More shouts came. The autofire stopped.

Lyons chanced a glance, pulled his head back instantly as slugs chipped concrete. He had seen fascists dashing into the open.

"I need a sideways periscope..." the ex-cop muttered to himself.

Gasoline roared, a yellow fireball rising above the traffic circle. Lyons's hand-radio buzzed.

"I see it!" Grimaldi told him. "Coming in, right now!"

"No! I'm—"

Autofire drowned out Lyons's voice. Booted feet ran around the corner. Lyons rolled, fired the G-3 like a pistol, felt the stock slam into his chest.

A fascist officer staggered back, clutching at the shaft of the flare protruding from his chest. Then the magnesium burst into chemical hell.

Lyons scrambled away, white light glaring, a hideous scream coming from the blazing soldier. Other fascists ran to the man's aid. Flicking the G-3's fire-selector down to full-auto, Lyons pointed the weapon and emptied the magazine. He saw men go down. Slamming in another magazine, he sprinted after the squad.

Slugs tore past him, then engine roar sounded in the sky. The night exploded in flames.

An incandescent chaos of screams and autofire surrounded him. The ammunition of cremated soldiers popped. Lyons dropped flat and squinted into the searing yellow wall.

Figures in flames fell thrashing, other soldiers ran silhouetted against the pyre of the offices. Lyons sighted and fired single bullets, dropping pursuers.

Hands grabbed him. He lashed out with a fist to hammer metal and flesh. A voice stopped him.

"*¡Amigo! Amigo. Vengo!*" A Salvadoran, perhaps five foot six, helped the hulking Lyons to his feet. The guerrilla had seen him fall and returned to help him.

Another Salvadoran sprayed slugs to cover the two retreating men. Engine roar passed over them again. Flamelight flashed in the barracks.

But the fascists pursued them. Lyons followed the others in the squad. They stumbled over the corpses of the Nazis they had killed on their way in. As bullets tore past, slamming into the prefab classrooms that covered them, Lyons heard Grimaldi call out over the radio again.

"Where are you? I got lots more to drop! Mark their positions and I'll—"

"The white flare!" Lyons shouted into his hand-radio. "Hit the white light!"

Lyons fitted the last flare onto the G-3. He checked the stenciled identification on the flare housing, saw the words for flare in three European languages. Then he stooped over a dead fascist and fired it into his chest.

As he sprinted away, white light flashed. Engine roar came from the night. The exploding av-gas seared Lyons's hair. Throwing himself behind the shelter of a classroom, he reloaded the G-3. He saw gray-uniformed soldiers, dropped each man with shots to their chests.

A blur of gray hit him. Hands closed on his throat. He knee-lifted the attacker, jerked the butt of the G-3 into the man's chin. He fired the bucking rifle into the downed fascist, plastic stabbing into his shoulder. The buttstock had broken off.

Lyons ran. A gray-uniformed soldier ran beside him, firing at the Salvadorans. Lyons swung the broken G-3 like a baseball bat into the soldier's face. Lyons did not stop to kill the screaming man. He unslung his Atchisson on the run.

A jeep roared up to the airfield gate, blocking the Salvadorans with a wild spray of fire from a pedestal-mounted M-60. Lyons saw his friends dive for cover.

Above him, he heard the engines of the DC-3. Aiming his Atchisson from the hip, he did not break stride. He ran straight at the jeep, snapping blasts from his auto-weapon. The standing machine gunner swiveled the M-60 at Lyons, then the man flew backward into the chain link fence, a gaping hole where a one-ounce slug had blown away his heart. Slugs smashed through the windshield of the jeep, the driver's right arm disappearing in a spray of gore, a rifleman in the passenger's seat losing his head, the jeep careering away.

Lyons dropped the magazine out of his autoshotgun, reloaded on the run, then sprawled flat on the asphalt and scanned the approach for gray uniforms. Salvadorans ran past him. He saw Blancanales, then Gadgets.

A hundred meters away, headlights raced toward the gate, autoweapons flashing from the sides. Lyons sprayed a blast of steel shot, then a bag fell from the sky, av-gas bursting in front of the fascists, a whoosh of petroflame instantly incinerating the men in the open jeep. Beyond the burning fascists, pillars of flame blazed upward.

Lyons screamed to the others, "Count everyone! Everyone with us?"

Blood sprayed with his words. He tasted the blood. Internal wounds.

Betrayed in Washington, battered beyond what any man could bear, pushed now to the furthest wall, Carl Lyons prepared to die. But life—the living in the midst of the dead—would not let him go.

"Specialist!"

Lyons squinted into the flames. Floyd Jefferson staggered from the smoke and shadows, one leg bloody. Floyd turned and sprayed rounds from his M-16, then lurched a few more steps and fell. Lyons groaned, raised himself and ran in agony to the journalist. He jerked him to his feet by his camera strap.

"Easy man! That's my equipment you're—"

One-handed, Lyons triggered a point-blank 12-gauge blast into the chest of a fascist.

"Can you run?" Lyons asked, blood filling his throat, his nasal passages.

Before Floyd could reply, Lyons whipped around, saw a gray form shouldering a rifle. Able Team's iron crazyman fired one-handed again, then fell in pain and rolled on the asphalt. He saw Floyd snapping photos of the inferno. He scrambled to his feet, lurched to the bleeding journalist and dragged him along with him.

Ahead, he saw his partners leading the group through the hole in the security fences. Lyons put his hand-radio to lips cherry red with blood.

"Eagle! We're going out the perimeter. Do the place. Do it all! Burn it!"

"Burn, baby, burn!" Floyd raved as if in fever, snapping more photos. "Did I get my hundred dollars' worth!"

"What are you talking about?"

"I had to pay one of those Salvadorans to stay behind," Floyd said, limping next to Lyons toward the darkness of the fence. "Portrait of a warrior's last stand! Boy, did I get what I came for."

"I didn't," grunted Lyons, pausing for his eyes to adjust to the darkness at the gate.

"No?"

"Quesada's in there somewhere."

They slipped through the fence and followed the glowing blue line through the darkness. Floyd pointed back to the Nazi base. Flames soared high into the night. He laughed.

"Even odds Quesada's in Hell right now," he said. "And if he isn't—"

The young reporter stopped a moment for emphasis. "He's got *you* after him," he smiled, standing against a backdrop of fire, "for as long as he lives. And that, my friend, is exactly the same thing."

Statement on Stivers

Dick Stivers has made the Able Team series one of the great success stories of modern publishing. His writing is way up there in the big league, alongside such major talent as Gar Wilson, Don Pendleton, Jerry Ahern and Jack Hild.

But Dick Stivers adds a new dimension to the concept of "writer." Dick lives his work. Literally. The first time he was shot at, and the first time he ever shot back, was in the streets of Los Angeles; since then, he has devoted his talent to telling how it really is in America and the world. He writes with complete integrity and breathtaking realism. Police departments consider Stivers "a man of honesty who cooperates in assisting to eliminate crime problems." Meanwhile Stivers hails friends with telegrams from distant parts: "Just climbed to the summit in a snowstorm. Transcendent experience. Almost died."

The Stivers legend continues. This month he writes to Gold Eagle from Panajachel, Guatemala: "I might disappear. I love it here. Today I came across three lovely young girls washing clothes. Despite their difficult lives, their classic, wood-colored features remained calm. They did not hear me until I said 'Beunas tardes.' All heads whipped around in shock and fear masked their faces. It was too much for me. I decided to return the way I had come. Then I saw the men with machetes, the men who are the 'unknown ones,' *los desconocidos*, assassins who slaughter whole towns. . . . "

Stivers will always survive, because he knows the way. He knows how to get that extra pound of strength out of life, even as the whole world falls to hell. Could it be that Dick Stivers is Carl Lyons?

ABLE TEAM

AN EXECUTIONER SERIES

#10 Royal Flush

MORE GREAT ACTION COMING SOON!

Able Team's mission: a cocaine bust in Manhattan.
But a crooked trail soon takes the three aces of death to
England, where the dignity of an ancient land is
fractured by atrocities so appalling that only Able
Team can smash through the nightmare to restore
stability.

Stony Man agent Leo Turrin is already there, and he
needs help. He gets it in Able Team's familiar style as
the American warriors blitz their way to the heart of
the horror.

No quarter is spared. Justice by fire, worldwide!

"Your blood will race on every page!"
—*New Breed*

JOIN FORCES WITH MACK BOLAN AND HIS NEW COMBAT TEAMS!

Mail this coupon today!